THIS BOOK

BELONGS TO

_____

Fairy Haven and the Quest for the Wand

GAIL CARSON LEVINE

Fairy Haven
and the
Quest
for the
Wand

illustrated by

DAVID CHRISTIANA

Disney PRESS
NEW YORK

Text by Gail Carson Levine
Art by David Christiana
Copyright © 2007 Disney Enterprises, Inc.

For information address
Disney Press, 114 Fifth Avenue,
New York, New York 10011-5690.

Library of Congress Cataloging-in-Publication Data on file.
ISBN 978-1-4231-3082-6
V381-8386-5-10015

Printed in the United States of America
First Disney Press paperback edition, 2010
1 3 5 7 9 10 8 6 4 2

VISIT: WWW.DISNEYFAIRIES.COM

SUSTAINABLE FORESTRY INITIATIVE

Certified Chain of Custody
Promoting Sustainable
Forest Management
www.sfiprogram.org

PWC-SFICOC-260

To my friend,
Joan Abelove
—g. c. l.

To Basil,
with apologies to Thaddeus
—d. c.

Soop's Song

(Accompanied by tail thumps against a hard surface
to establish a slow, sad rhythm)

Ui eEe... ooooioooOooo

aiiyoyo!

yuyuUyuy...aAaAaA Eaa.

  aaE   eee!

ooooioooOooo. iAii...

iU eI aOaO!

uuooo... uUooo...o

  uaeouuaeou yooeee!

iaia.   ooooioooOooo

yuyuUyuy ayAy!

ioiOioi EE

ee...Ee eE...ieieYooyoo!

    iii

    ooooioooOooo yuyuUyuy eeay!

eaea uaueu u U u

oooooioooOooo!

oooooioooOooo

  oo... OO ooeyyaya!

yuyuUyuy. iAii...

iU eI....ooeeO!

  ieieYooyoo. EE ee

  iAii Uyaya!

ooeyyaya...

oooooioooOooo iiEeO!

(*Translation from the Mermish*: Once upon a time, more or less recently, a beautiful and generous mermaid of middle rank met a tiny and insignificant fairy, who was so lowly she lacked both wings and a wand. And she certainly had no tail, since fairies are not fortunate in this regard. The fairy most pathetically begged the kindhearted mermaid for the gift of her comb, a four-pearled whalebone of superb design. The comb was needed, or so the cunning fairy said, to save the life of a bird whose survival was of no concern to mermaids. However, because of her great goodness, the lovely mermaid consented, asking only for a magic wand in return. The lying, ungrateful fairy agreed and swam away with the precious comb—NEVER TO RETURN WITH THE MAGIC WAND—although the sweet mermaid waited, first with hope, then with resignation, and finally with despair. She composed this tragic and moving song to express her regret at the treachery of fairies.)

Fairy Haven
and the
Quest
for the
Wand

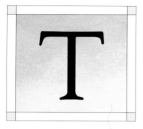HE MERMAIDS dived when Rani approached, flying in on Brother Dove's back. It broke Rani's heart to see them go. She was a water-talent fairy, and she loved mermaids.

Only the mermaid Soop remained, treading water just long enough to see that Rani had brought no wand. Then she dived, too.

"Wait!" Rani shouted as Brother Dove landed on Marooners' Rock. "I want you to have a wand. Mother Dove won't let me—"

It was too late. Rani was talking to Soop's tail, just as she had yesterday and the day before and the day before that.

She told Brother Dove to leave her. Alone on Marooners' Rock, she wept. Because of her talent, she wept often, sweated easily, and her nose tended to run.

After drying her eyes on a leafkerchief, she kicked off her sensible walking shoes and slipped into the lagoon. Of all fairies, Rani was the only one who could swim, and that was because she had no wings to drag her under.

When she tired of floating and splashing, she made a play mermaid out of water. It was too bad the real mermaids hadn't stayed to see. The water mermaid seemed to have scaly skin, its fingernails were tiny fins, and it was almost as graceful as a real mermaid. Rani even gave it a long pink scarf, just like Soop's.

Rani swam with the imitation mermaid, but she couldn't make its tail swish. Worse, its eyes were empty, and its smile never varied. In the end, she turned it into a pyramid of bubbles.

If only she had a wand for Soop!

Rani had no illusions. The wand wouldn't make Soop like

her. Mermaids looked down on fairies, and a fulfilled promise wouldn't change that.

But first Rani would use the wand to make Soop her friend. Then she'd hand it over and everything would be lovely.

Brother Dove came for Rani at sunset. The lagoon is perilous at night, because the mermaids sing their most magical songs then. Pirates see dead sea captains. Birds fly upside down. Fairies turn into bats.

For her part, Soop was enraged. She'd given Rani a comb in exchange for a wand, and she wanted the wand. She had plans for it.

She was convinced Rani was taunting her by returning to the lagoon every day without it. Soop wanted to vent her anger, but fairies were beneath her, so for a month after the hurricane she did nothing.

Finally, one night, she was too angry to sing. The next morning, she didn't dive when Rani arrived.

Rani was thrilled. Her glow flared. She wept happy tears. "Oh, Soop! Oh, Soop!" She wanted to say the fascinating things she'd practiced for this moment, about swimming and fish fins and underwater castles. "Oh, Soop!"

Soop smiled pleasantly until Brother Dove left. Then she reared up so that she was balanced precariously on the tip of her tail. The smile vanished. "You promised! You promised, and I have waited. I've waited patiently." This wasn't true. She'd been angry since the first day. "When will you fulfill your promise?" She flopped back down on Marooners' Rock and whispered menacingly, "Beware a mermaid's wrath!"

Rani dabbed at the seawater and sweat on her face with a leafkerchief. "I want you to have it, but—"

"If you want me to have it," Soop said, "why don't I have—"

"—it? I'd need to get it." The only other time they'd met, Rani had told Soop that Never fairies didn't have wands. They had fairy dust and Mother Dove. "But Mother Dove won't let me."

Excuses! "Observe, little fairy." Soop beckoned the water below.

"My name is Rani." She smiled ingratiatingly.

Automatically, Soop said, "I am Soop." Then she frowned. She didn't want to be polite. "It doesn't matter what your name is. Watch the water."

It lapped higher and higher on the rock, up to the hem of Rani's skirt.

"Fulfill your promise. Bring a wand to our castle. The water is rising in your Fairy—"

"—Haven. Don't!" Rani's water talent wasn't strong enough

to dry up a flood. Not even the combined talents of every water-talent fairy would be strong enough.

A flood would destroy Fairy Haven.

"Oh, don't!"

"Bring me a wand!" Soop dived.

OTHER DOVE was in her nest on her egg. As usual, she was attended by Beck, the island's most skilled animal-talent fairy. Queen Clarion, or Ree as her fairies called her, was there, too, describing the final repairs to the Home Tree following the hurricane.

Rani stepped from Brother Dove's back onto the edge of the nest. "Mother Dove! Soop is going to flood Fairy Haven! Now we have to give her a wand."

Rani noticed that the ground was dry. Soop might have changed her mind, but Rani didn't mention this possibility.

Mother Dove was aware that Rani was leaving something out, and she knew why—it was that wand again.

Mother Dove had refused to let anyone go to the mainland for a wand because wands were dangerous. She wouldn't put fairies at risk. Staying alive was more important than keeping promises.

But now . . . a flood!

Beck held up a hand. "Listen!"

Ree cocked her head, and her golden tiara slipped over one ear. "I don't hear anything."

Beck flew down and returned, cradling a worm. "See how upset he—"

"—is." To Rani, the worm just looked hairy and floppy—and damp.

"He says water falling from above is one thing, but this is rising from below. It's frightening him."

Mother Dove patted her egg with a wing. Never fear, my love, she thought. Mother isn't afraid.

But she was. A flood would be disastrous.

Ree said, "I'm afraid we have to get the wand." She sounded grim, although she was secretly pleased. A few waves of a wand, just a few, would turn Fairy Haven into fairy heaven.

Mother Dove sensed Ree's pleasure and was more worried than ever. Ree was generally such a cautious, levelheaded queen. Mother Dove understood the allure of a wand. She herself had a wish that only a wand could grant, a wish that she would never make. But oh, how she would love to make it.

Wishes, tantalizing wishes, made wands dangerous. A fairy might make the tiniest, most innocent wish, and it could cause a world of trouble. Mother Dove doubted even she could see around all the corners of a wish.

Besides, a wand could bring out the worst in anyone, even a Never fairy: greed, jealousy, selfishness.

And who knew what Soop would wish for?

"I'll go to Tutupia," Ree said. Tutupia ruled the Great Wanded fairies.

Mother Dove nodded reluctantly. They couldn't allow Fairy Haven to be flooded, and Ree's authority would have weight with the Great Wandies. "Take Rani."

"Me?" Rani's mouth watered. She'd get her wish!

"Yes," Mother Dove said. "You know Soop. That will be helpful."

"Mother Dove?" Beck said. "Can I go?"

Beck wants the wand, too! Mother Dove thought, disheartened. "No, dear. The animals will need you. Ree, take—"

"Tink?" Rani said.

"—a balloon carrier. Brother Dove needn't go."

Ree nodded, although she hadn't pulled a carrier in years.

"And you can bring the wand back in it." Mother Dove cooed, "Yes, Rani, Tink should go, too." Tink had discipline.

Or, Mother Dove thought, Tink usually had discipline. In the face of a wand, even Tink might give way.

Ree left the nest to arrange for the balloon carrier and to give instructions for fighting the coming flood. Brother Dove took Rani to the Home Tree to tell Tink about the new quest, the quest for the wand.

As soon as they were gone, Althea, a scout, flew to the nest. "Mother Dove, may I go for the wand, too? I can watch for hawks."

"No, dear. I need you to protect the fairies who will be fighting the flood."

Althea left, flying low out of disappointment.

Next, a keyhole designer asked to go for the wand, then two cricket whistlers, followed by a walnut drummer. They each nodded when Mother Dove said no, but she felt their discontent.

Mother Dove brushed a feather along her egg. She thought, I'm glad you have nothing to wish for, my love.

But did it? she wondered. Did it wish to emerge and fly?

Vidia hovered near the nest, seeming to arrive out of nowhere. "Darling . . ."

"Fly with you, Vidia," Mother Dove said, giving the traditional Never fairy greeting.

"Dearest, I can fetch the wand faster than anyone. Especially—"

Mother Dove cooed in an unusually high pitch. Three scouts swooped down on Vidia and carried her away. Vidia was the fastest of the fast-flying talents, and if the scouts hadn't surprised her, they never would have been able to catch her.

She, who was loyal to no one, felt betrayed. She kicked and flapped her wings, but the scouts held on.

Mother Dove called after her, "If your wish came true it would break your heart." In spite of everything, Mother Dove loved Vidia.

Vidia's shouts diminished in the distance.

"Mother Dove?" A fairy turned an aerial cartwheel and landed on the branch below the nest.

Mother Dove cooed, and Prilla did a handstand. She loved Mother Dove's voice.

"Yes, Prilla."

"Can I go on the new quest?"

"Do you want to wave the wand, too?"

"No . . . Yes . . . I mean, better cartwheels would be nice, but

I just want to go." The other quest had been thrilling, and Prilla's two favorite fairies, Rani and Tink, were going.

Mother Dove smiled. At least one fairy hadn't been infected by the wand—yet. "You'd better not, dear. If there were more clapping-talent fairies, it would be different."

Prilla nodded solemnly. She was the only one who could save fairies from death when Clumsy—that is, human—children stopped believing.

"And we'll need everyone's help against the flood," Mother Dove added.

"I'll help!" Prilla somersaulted off the branch and started for the Home Tree.

Another fairy landed on the spot Prilla had just left. "A dairy talent might come in handy on the mainland."

Mother Dove said she didn't think so and waited for the next request, which came a minute later. And then there was another, and one after that. The wand was still across the ocean, but its influence had already arrived.

THREE

HEN RANI stepped into Tink's inside-a-teakettle workshop, Tink was repairing a saucepan that had been brought to her by Terence, a dust talent. He was at her side, watching.

Rani had never seen a pot in such desperate straits. Its sides were down. Its bottom was one bump after another. Its handle hung by a thread. Its finish was past thinking of.

"I left it on the stove too long," Terence had said when he'd presented it to Tink. "I'd fly backward if I could for damaging it."

This was the fairy equivalent of an apology, although he wasn't really sorry, and he hadn't left the pan on the stove too long, either. He'd placed it under a tree and had rained rocks down on it for hours. After that he'd attacked it with a hammer and had soaked it in vinegar. All so he could present Tink with a problem worthy of her attention—and have an excuse for visiting her.

Rani coughed when she came in, knowing Tink hated interruptions.

Tink whirled around, her hand on her bangs. "What?"

"We have to go to Mother Dove now." Rani explained every-thing. "We're leaving Never Land right away."

Tink put down the pot. A wand! A flood! A wand!

Terence was frightened for Tink. A trip to the mainland was arduous, and the Great Wandies were known to be harebrained. "You'll need fairy dust."

He flew out of the workshop. As he left, he thought about what he would wish for if he ever held the wand. One wish, only one, and then he'd never want anything more ever again.

A supply of fairy dust was already in the carrier when he arrived at the nest with a full satchel. He put his in, too, just in case.

A crowd of fairies clustered in Mother Dove's tree, each fairy hoping to be needed at the last minute.

Terence told Tink, "Keep a sharp eye out for hawks."

She pulled her bangs. Of course she would.

The afternoon was mild, as they mostly are on the island. The sun shone. Mother Dove's branch was dry. But the ground was squishy.

"The Great Wandies are rash," Mother Dove said, although she hated to speak ill of any sort of fairy. "Ree, take care."

Ree nodded. "Rani will stay out of the way until it's—"

"—safe. All right."

"Ree . . . Rani . . . Tink . . ." Mother Dove cooed after each name. She hesitated. "Try not to wave the wand, but if you must wave it, make only one wish and make it a small wish, an unimportant one."

She knew they might not be able to honor their promises, and she also knew they'd hate themselves if they couldn't. Still, their pledges might strengthen them.

They promised, although Tink tugged her bangs. Didn't Mother Dove trust her not to make a foolish wish?

Mother Dove saw Tink's irritation.

Rani was annoyed, too. She couldn't remember ever being annoyed with Mother Dove before. Her wish for friendship with Soop seemed small, but she didn't know what Mother Dove would think. She was close to tears, and the last thing Fairy Haven needed was more water.

Mother Dove's voice grew stern. "Don't use the wand to end the flood. Ree, don't let the Great Wandies do it, either. Soop will retaliate. She could send a tidal wave." Mother Dove shivered. "She could send sharks."

Everyone shivered.

Tink said, "Couldn't we stop Soop from wanting to flood us?" That seemed harmless enough.

"Yes, Tink, you could." Mother Dove's voice had never sounded so cold, so unloving.

Tink—brave Tink—was terrified.

"And someone," Mother Dove continued in that same awful tone, "could wave a wand and stop you from wanting to fix pots." She saw Tink's tremulous glow and cooed.

Rani stepped into the balloon carrier. Tink, her glow still wavery from Mother Dove's rebuke, felt for the knife on her belt.

Ree picked up the carrier's towing cord and proclaimed, "We will be careful. We will be kind. We will be Never fairies at our best."

The quest was on.

HAT NIGHT, while the questers were on the first leg of their journey, Soop sang in the lagoon, a song about vengeance.

In the Home Tree, fairies were consumed by wand wishes. Dulcie, a baking-talent fairy, dreamed of wanding a new flavor into existence: richer than chocolate, livelier than mint, fruitier than fruit cocktail. Bess, the island's leading artist, dreamed of brushstrokes like lightning forks and paints as pure as new souls.

Terence tossed and turned, trying to frame a wish that would lead Tink to care for him, naturally, without forcing her feelings. He flew to the beach, where he stared out over the waves and decided that if he had a wand right then, he'd wish only for her safe return.

Vidia, shut up in Rani's empty bedroom, sat utterly still. The door was locked from the other side, and a scout was posted there. The two windows, round as the portholes of a ship, were shuttered. The windows had no locks, but two scouts were stationed outside each one. Vidia tried to ignore the drip-drip-drip from Rani's ceiling into a tub where Minnie, Rani's pet minnow, swam. Vidia needed to think.

Russell, a scout whose right wing had no glow, didn't wish for completeness. Instead, he wished to be Mother Dove's favorite out of all the Never fairies.

His wish woke Mother Dove, who shed a tear for him and then couldn't fall back to sleep. Instead, she fretted about her own wish. Finally, she indulged herself and imagined waving a wand.

A moment later, she'd feel movement. She'd raise herself up, ready to descend if she was mistaken. But then she'd hear a faint scratching. She'd move aside and perch next to her darling egg. A thin jagged line would be etched in it. Another line would appear, and another, then a fissure. The hatching would be underway, unstoppable.

A shudder would run through Never Land. Mother Dove would lose her wisdom and become an ordinary dove. Her molted feathers would no longer make fairy dust. The egg's magic would be over, too, and so would the magic of the island itself, the magic that kept age away.

The chick would emerge. Mother Dove's baby would look like any other dove chick, a fistful of wet straw with big eyes, an outsize beak, and a bewildered expression. So beautiful. So beautiful.

Mother Dove smiled sadly. The island needed its magic. The fairies needed her. She'd never wave the wand. She settled down to sleep.

The questers flew on toward the mainland. Their trip took two days, and meanwhile, the floodwaters rose.

Queen Tutupia was in her castle ballroom leading her entourage in the royal wand ballet. Unnoticed, Ree and Tink fluttered in the doorway, waiting for the dance to end. They had a Never fairy's notion of manners—no manners at all, by most standards—and they would have flown in anyway. But the Great Wandies kept leaping up unexpectedly, waving their arms and beating their wings. It was safer to wait.

Ree and Tink had been following Tutupia for hours, having doors slammed in their faces, being drowned out by the Great Wandy orchestra. And the last time, Tutupia had vanished as soon as they'd drawn close. It had taken half an hour to find her again. Both Ree and Tink were conscious that Rani, who was waiting outside the castle, would be wild with worry by now.

And the flood would be deeper than ever.

The ballroom was blindingly bright. The floor was white marble. Each of the dozen crystal chandeliers had as many arms as an octopus, and each arm ended in five lights. The walls were mirrors separated by gold columns studded with diamonds.

Tutupia raised her arms slowly, her golden wand in her right hand. She was seven feet tall, with four-foot-long flowing red hair. With her arms raised, her wings spread, and her hooped skirt she was twice as big as the mill that ground the fairy dust back in Fairy Haven.

Following her lead, the entourage raised their arms slowly. Tutupia folded her wings and began to pirouette. The entourage folded their wings and pirouetted, too. Faster and faster they spun.

Tutupia lowered her arms. Her spinning slowed. She sank to the ballroom floor and tucked her head under her wing.

At last it's over, Ree thought. She nodded at Tink, and the two flew side by side toward Tutupia.

Tutupia didn't see them. She raised her arms again. The entourage raised their arms. Tutupia dropped her arms. A Great Wandy arm conked Ree and Tink on the head, knocking both fairies to the floor.

Rani paced up and down below the balloon carrier, which was tethered to a tree branch. She couldn't decide whether to stay put or to set off in search of Ree and Tink, who might need rescuing. But even at a dead run, it could take her days, maybe weeks, to find them.

In a week they'd be past rescuing.

In a week Fairy Haven could be at the bottom of a lake. She'd never missed her wings so much.

When the dance of the Great Wanded fairies really ended, the Great Wandies left the ballroom. No one saw Ree or Tink stretched out on the floor, unconscious.

Ree woke up first. There was her tiara, a few inches away. She put the crown on slightly askew, to avoid a bump on her head, which throbbed painfully. "Tink?"

Tink lay face down, two feet away.

"Tink!" Could she be—"Tink!" Ree ran to her and knelt. "Wake up!" She rolled Tink over.

Tink's eyes opened. "Are they gone?"

"Yes. I just woke up, too. I wonder how long we were out."

Tink shrugged. "Where do you think they went?"

Of course Ree didn't know, although she felt she should. They spent another hour flying through hallways and flitting in and out of rooms before they discovered Tutupia and her entourage in the dining room.

They flew in, unconcerned about interrupting a meal, and landed between Tutupia's gold wand and a scallion roll almost as tall as they were.

Ree began. "Your Royal Highness . . ."

Tutupia had just taken in a mouthful of cranberry juice. She sputtered. Ree's long, blue skirt and Tink's legs were drenched. But at least their wings stayed dry.

"Fufalla!" Tutupia cried. "No pranks at dinner!"

Ree shook out her skirt. "I am Queen—"

"Fufalla! Stop!"

Tink tugged her bangs. "We're Never fairies from—"

Fufalla, the Great Wandy three seats from Tutupia, said, "I didn't do anything."

Ree realized first: Tutupia thought they were a figment of Fufalla's wand! "I'm a queen! Like you! See my—"

"Fuff, we've gone over this."

"I didn't make them," Fufalla said, "but I can make them disappear."

"We're real!" Tink shouted. "I can prove it!" How could she prove it?

Tutupia sighed. "Yes?"

"We come from Never Land."

"This is tiresome, Fuff."

"We need your aid," Ree said. "We're desperate."

"They would say something like that." Tutupia picked up her wand.

"Don't!" Tink flew sideways.

Ree, who was faster, flew straight up. The wand missed her, but it got Tink, who disappeared.

REE FLEW above the heads of the Great Wandies, looking for Tink, who had been thinned out to invisibility. She was so sparse, Ree could fly right through her and feel nothing.

Tink barely noticed Ree. She was too busy trying to pull herself together, trying to become compact enough to be seen again. She'd become almost as interesting as a broken pot. She'd mend herself. She was sure she was making progress.

Of course, she wasn't. She was powerless against a wand in the hands of a Great Wandy.

Ree flew out of the dining hall to check the corridor, in case Tink had escaped. No Tink. How dare Tutupia vaporize a fairy! She flew back in but stayed near the door. "You have no—"

Tutupia raised her wand again.

Ree whooshed out the door, leaving dignity behind. She decided to go to Rani. Maybe Rani would have an idea.

"Ree!" Rani cried. "What took—where's Tink?"

Ree told her.

Tink? Gone? Rani was beyond tears. "We have to go to them. Ree, take me."

But Ree didn't want to endanger Rani. "I'll go."

"If you won't take me, I'll walk, and someone will step on me, and you'll have my squished self on your conscience."

Ree flew back in with Rani in the balloon carrier and shouted, "How dare—"

"—you!" Rani yelled. "We're real! Look at me! I have no wings. See! I'm a fairy without—"

But it was the balloon carrier that did the trick. The Great Wandies hadn't seen one of them before, and Tutupia didn't think Fufalla clever enough to have wanded it up.

Tutupia said, "Is it possible?"

"I told you I didn't do anything," Fufalla said.

"Did anyone else?"

Each fairy shook her head.

"Oh, dear," Tutupia said, standing. "I'm sorry. It was a—"

"Make Tink reappear!" Ree roared.

"Immediately!" Rani thundered.

Tutupia waved her wand.

There was Tink, tugging her bangs. "I was getting it. You didn't have to do that."

Ree brought the balloon carrier down on the tablecloth. The carrier would have been bigger than a Great Wandy

serving platter, if there had been any serving platters.

A Great Wandy said, "They're so cute!"

Never fairies hate being called cute. Ree drew herself up to her full five inches and straightened her tiara in spite of the bump on her head. "I'm Queen Clarion." She didn't curtsy. Never fairies usually don't, and she was a queen besides. "You may call me *Ree*."

Tutupia said, "It is an honor to meet you, Queen Ree."

Ree answered, as any Never fairy would, "I look forward to flying with you."

Someone said, "Look at her little fingers. And her tiny fingernails."

Ree put her hands behind her back. She introduced Tink and Rani and named their talents.

"Fly with you," Tink said.

"May we offer you some—"

"—food? We don't have time to eat," Rani said. They hadn't eaten anything since they'd left Fairy Haven.

Tutupia ignored Rani's refusal and raised her wand.

Tink and Ree zoomed upward. Rani trembled and perspired.

A Never-fairy-sized table appeared atop the gigantic one. Three place settings materialized, and three silver chairs drew themselves up to the table.

"What can we serve you?" Tutupia asked.

Perhaps Tutupia was a little deaf. Ree raised her voice. "We have no time for food. We have—"

Tutupia continued, "The hospitality of the Great Wanded fairies is legendary. What can we serve you?"

Ree gave up. "A cashew loaf. A dozen grains of purple rice, if you have it. Three roast peas. And a sliced raspberry for dessert."

"Ooo!" fifty fairies squealed delightedly.

"Adorable!" Tutupia said.

"And water," Rani added.

Tutupia waved her wand. The meal appeared on the table.

Tink was stunned. They didn't cook! They had no pots and pans! She looked around the big table. Each place setting was different, and each meal was different. Fifty wands had been waved to produce fifty dinners. At the end of the meal, fifty wands would make everything vanish. No dishes or pots to wash. No leftovers.

The Great Wandies have no meaning in their lives, Tink thought. They never have to fix a pot. They never have to do anything.

A pitcher set itself down on the table. Goblets arrived, too. Before Tink could pick up the pitcher, it rose in the air and poured boysenberry juice into the goblets.

"How nice." Rani hated boysenberry juice.

They began to eat, although they felt awkward with all those enormous eyes scrutinizing every chew. They hurried through the meal. Even Tink hurried, although she usually chewed every bite twenty times.

When she finished, Rani mopped her face with her napkin.

Ree put down her fork and stood. "Your Highness—"

Tutupia held up her hand. "Now you must rest, Your Majesty. We won't discuss anything until you've had a good sleep."

"Your journey must have been exhausting," Fufalla said. "How long was—"

"—it? Two days, but—"

"Two days!" Tutupia said. She'd never flown for even two hours. When she left the castle, her wand took her wherever she wanted to go. "You certainly must rest."

"Yes, we must," Tink agreed. She added cleverly, "But since we're so small, we need little sleep."

A Great Wandy said, "They're precious!"

"We generally sleep for eight minutes," Ree said, "which last us a whole—"

"—day. We can sleep while you eat dessert."

More than eight minutes passed before the Great Wandies wanded up beds in a corner of the dining room. First they debated the colors of the canopies on the four-posters (mauve, chartreuse, and daffodil), the number of pillows (three per bed), and the sort of feathers in the pillows (hummingbird).

At last, the questers climbed in, intending to feign sleep. Ree removed her tiara and fell into a dreamless slumber, while Rani plunged into a nightmare of angry purple mermaids in a boysenberry ocean.

Luckily, Tink stayed awake, doggedly counting to sixty eight times over. When she finished, she sat up and stretched in case the Great Wandies were watching, which they were, avidly.

Ree was snoring, and Rani's head was buried in her pillow. Tink woke them. A Great Wandy lifted Rani onto the table. Ree and Tink flew to stand next to her.

Tutupia said, "You have come a long way for an important reason, I'm sure. How may we help you?"

Ree felt ridiculous for being nervous. She was a queen! "We . . . We . . ." She took a deep breath. "Er, we must have a wand."

Fifty fairies laughed.

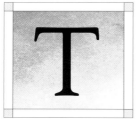UTUPIA SAID, "I thought Never fairies had enchanted dirt. Why—"

"Dust, not dirt!" Ree said. "Fairy—"

"—dust. We don't need the wand for ourselves. We need it for a mermaid named Soop."

"'Soup'?" Tutupia chuckled. "Why not 'Sandwich'?"

"We only call her Soop," Rani said, feeling indignant. "Her Mermish name is much longer and more beautiful."

Peter Pan had dubbed her Soop, and the fairies had adopted it, too.

"Why does she need a—"

"—wand?" Rani explained that the wand had been promised in exchange for help saving Mother Dove and Never Land's magic.

Ree said, "Soop has begun to flood Fairy Haven. She won't stop until she gets her wand."

Fufalla said, "I can settle Soop."

"No!" Rani cried.

"We must keep our promise," Ree said.

"Soop won't be able to control one of our wands," Tutupia said. "You won't be able to, either. Sometimes we can barely control them. They're frisky. They can be mischievous."

Ree thought Tutupia had no idea what a Never fairy was capable of.

"A wild wand could do anything," Fufalla said. "Flooding might be the least of it."

"Our wands aren't evil," Tutupia added, "but some are better than others. Some aren't nice, especially if they have a small heart and an impish mind."

Fascinating! Tink thought. Pots had personalities, too.

Tutupia continued, "Occasionally, the wands simply don't understand us. If a wand turns you upside down, it doesn't know you don't like being that way. If you struggle, it thinks you're playing with it."

Ree thought, We'll have to go to the Lesser Wandies.

"The Lesser Wandies' wands are worse than ours," Fufalla said. "Theirs have absolutely no sense of decorum, and they all have small hearts and mean minds."

Tink wondered if they could find a wand somewhere else.

Tutupia said, "We can stop your flood. We can make Fairy Haven bone dry."

Fufalla said, "We can make Soop forget she was ever promised anything. We can turn your mermaids into whales."

"It would be fun," Tutupia said. "We can—"

"No!" Rani cried.

"Don't trouble yourselves," Ree added.

"No trouble," Fufalla said. "We simply wave our wands."

Tink said, "Do you have any wands that are too old to be frisky?"

"No . . ." Tutupia looked thoughtful. "But perhaps we could put a wand to sleep."

"Will it work if it's asleep?" Rani asked.

"It's a wand!" Fufalla said. "It makes magic, even in its sleep."

"Asleep," Tutupia said, "it will do exactly as it's told."

"Wonderful!" Ree said. "Perfect. May we have one?"

"The generosity of the Great Wanded fairies is legendary." Tutupia held out her hand, palm up. "Come, Never fairies. You can pick your wand."

Rani climbed onto Tutupia's cushiony palm.

"You, too," Tutupia told Tink and Ree. "It will be faster." She flew them out of the dining room. As they glided through the corridors, she said, "You will use the wand before you give it to Soop. You won't be able to resist."

This irritated Tink. She could resist, if she wanted to.

"Use caution with your wishes. Tell your mermaid to use caution, too." Tutupia brought the three fairies up to her face as she flew. Her expression was solemn. "Wand madness can overcome you. The temptation to wave a wand and get the things you've always wanted, the things you couldn't achieve any other way, is hard to withstand. It happens to us, too."

The fairies heard *plink-plinks*.

"Listen to the wands wriggle and ring," Tutupia said. "Isn't it pretty?"

She flew toward double doors that opened as she approached. Within, wands in trays squirmed on a round mahogany table. Some wands were gold, some silver, some copper, some brass, some pewter.

Tutupia ran her hand over a tray. "Aren't they pretty?"

Tink thought they were. They were metal, after all.

Ree said, "Why aren't they making mischief?" No one was controlling them now.

"They can't do anything unless someone holds them. Oh, they can wiggle a bit, nothing more."

"Can I touch one?" Tink asked, eager to see how potlike they were.

"Better not until you pick one, and I put it to—"

"—sleep. Are these your spares?"

"These are our new wands, little Rani. Young fairies find their first wands here, and sometimes an experienced fairy wants a change."

Ree and Tink flew over the wands. Rani picked her way between the trays. Some wands were plain metal sticks, but others were encrusted with jewels. A few were a yard long. Most were about fifteen inches. Several were considerably shorter.

"When I put the wand to sleep," Tutupia said, "it will obey commands, but it won't be able to reverse them. Sleeping wands can't. It's too confusing for them. So if Soop, or anyone else, commands the wand to do something, the command will be permanent."

"Can an awake wand reverse a command?" Tink asked.

"Yes. But an awake wand won't obey Soop or any of you. It will obey only one of us. So Soop's commands will be irreversible. Make sure she understands that."

"How does she give a command?" Ree asked.

"She must think what she wants very clearly, and the wording must be exact because a sleeping wand will do precisely what it's told. An awake wand with a big heart and an easy mind will make allowances and grant its wielder's true wish, but a sleeping wand won't be able to."

"I see," Ree said. Wands were complicated.

"Sometimes it helps to say the command out loud, to get the wording right. Then Soop must wave the wand."

Tink enjoyed every new rule.

"An awake wand has to suit its wielder," Tutupia said. "A

fairy may audition a dozen wands before she finds one that's right for her. The wand and its wielder needn't be alike, either. A generous fairy, for example, may be well served by a stingy wand."

A stingy wand! Tink thought, marveling.

"Even a disagreeable wand can find its fairy, but . . ." Tutupia clasped her hands rapturously. ". . . there's nothing better than a bighearted wand. I do hope you choose one with a big heart. I hope, I hope, I hope." Her tone turned practical. "Since these particular wands have never been used, I can't tell you about their characters."

Rani passed a gold wand with copper stripes. She wanted to pick a good one, too, but she didn't know how to choose. They had nothing to go on. Maybe Soop would like a jeweled wand, or maybe not. Rani didn't care what metal the wand was made of, and the wand could be any size. The balloon carrier could accommodate the biggest wand here.

"Do any of them understand Mermish?" Tink asked.

"Wands understand every language."

That was no help. They felt rushed. The Home Tree might be flooded halfway up its trunk by now.

"Look at this one," Rani said, pointing.

Tink and Ree came to see. It was a thin silver wand, three inches long, with a squiggly engraving that ran its length. The

first thought they each had was that it was small enough for them to wave.

They didn't see how reckless its squiggle was, how peppy its shine. Of course they couldn't see its character—its mind, which thrummed with mischief and a large dollop of spite, or its weak, chilly heart.

They paid no attention to the silver wand's neighbor, a brass wand that was three inches longer. It was a far better choice, with a loose curve and a relaxed air, a kindly heart and a tolerant mind.

The questers invented reasons for their preference. Rani told herself that the silver wand's squiggle looked like ocean spray, which Soop would enjoy. Tink thought its size would make it easier to examine. Ree felt virtuous for judging that a smaller, lighter wand would shorten the trip home.

They were already in the grip of wand madness.

Ree said, "We'll take this one."

They couldn't have made a worse choice.

ANI FORGOT she wasn't supposed to touch. She picked up the small silver wand to see how heavy it was—but it had other ideas.

It rose into the air.

She was flying again! For a moment she was exhilarated. Then the wand bucked. It jerked. She was above it. She was below. She was sideways.

She shrieked and attempted to straddle the wand, but it was flipping about too much.

Tutupia plucked it out of the air and set Rani back down on the table.

"Are you all right?" Ree cried.

Rani nodded, gasping for breath.

Tink asked, "What was it—"

"—like? Strong!"

"Are you a strong little wand?" Tutupia sniffed the wand and stroked it. She licked it. She rolled it between her palms. It jumped and jiggled. She murmured, "Will you be good to the little fairies and the mermaid?"

She touched it with her own wand. Sparks flew between them. "Sleep. Sleeeeeep. Sleeeeeeeep, little wand."

The wand resisted as long as it could but finally gave in and slept.

"If anything goes wrong," Tutupia said, "let us know. Fuff and I will zip over to your Ever Land and set things right."

"Never Land," Ree said. "I'm sure all will be—"

"—well. Don't inconvenience yourselves."

"We'd be happy to come. Queen Ree, I'd love to see your itty-bitty queendom."

In her most regal manner, Ree replied, "Then you must come for a state visit . . . someday, when Fairy Haven can receive you properly."

Tutupia beamed. "Thank you." She waved her wand, and the balloon carrier appeared, floating above the wand table. She lifted Rani and placed her and the sleeping wand inside.

Ree said the Never fairy farewell: "Fly again soon."

Then Tink and Ree picked up the balloon-carrier cord and began to fly toward the door.

"What are you doing?" Tutupia cried, astonished.

"Going home." Tink tugged her bangs. She didn't know what she'd do if Tutupia delayed them again.

Tutupia laughed. "You have a wand now. It will take you home in a—"

"—flash." Rani felt foolish for not thinking of this.

Ree and Tink did, too. The wand could save Fairy Haven days of flooding.

"Who wants to try it out? Queen Ree, the honor is yours."

"Er . . ." Ree didn't want to do it. She intended to keep her pledge to Mother Dove to make only one wish, and she didn't want to use it up. "I'll pass the honor to Tink. Her talent is more suited to wands."

Tink didn't want to use up her wish, either. Feeling like a traitor, she said, "Rani can wave it. She should be the one to take us to the—"

"—lagoon." Rani looked reproachfully at Tink. "Queen Tutupia, could you wave your wand and send us home?"

"Certainly, I can." Tutupia shook her head. "I've never seen anything like you little fairies. Everybody else is itching to wave a wand."

"Mmm," Ree said.

Rani asked, "Could you send us to a particular spot on Never Land, the bank of Havendish Stream, just over the border of Fairy Haven?" They could each wave the wand there before going to the lagoon.

"Havendish Stream." Tutupia waved her wand in a grand gesture.

The Never fairies didn't move an inch.

Tutupia looked puzzled. She waved her wand again.

The Never fairies didn't budge.

Tutupia addressed her wand. "No tricks. I am your master." She waved it.

"Is your wand broken?" Tink said eagerly. Perhaps she could fix it. It would be the experience of a lifetime even to try.

Tutupia turned away from the fairies and waved her wand. A magnolia tree, laden with blossoms, filled the wand room, its trunk butting against the mahogany table.

Ree wondered if she should use her wish to replace the Home Tree with something showier, more impressive.

"My wand is being blocked," Tutupia said.

The questers knew only one force strong enough to block a wand: Never Land. It didn't want them to get there on a wand wave.

"I'll try one more time." Tutupia held the wand close to her lips. "Send these Never fairies to their Havendish Stream. Conquer impediments." She waved it.

Nothing happened.

Ree and Tink took up the balloon-carrier cord again and began to fly out of the room.

Tutupia frowned. Her wand hand twitched. She restrained herself and burst out, "Don't you puny fairies ever say *thank you?*"

Ree and Tink stopped flying and hovered.

"No, we don't," Tink said, unaware of Tutupia's anger. "Clumsies say—"

Ree saw Tutupia's frown deepen. "Of course we're very grateful to you. Without your help, our situation would have been hopeless. You have the gratitude of the Never fairies."

Tutupia was completely mollified. She waved her wand again, and a picnic basket appeared in the carrier. "In case you get hungry." A jug settled down next to the basket. "In case you get—"

"—thirsty. You've equipped us marvelously," Rani said, hoping to forestall more cargo.

But the compliment went to Tutupia's head. She added pillows, blankets, and books. Rani moved over to make room for everything.

"Mementos of the queen of the Great Wanded fairies."

Mercifully, the shower of gifts stopped. Tink and Ree began to pull the carrier cord. Tutupia said farewell.

The questers flew out of the castle. Tink and Ree put all their strength into their wing muscles, but they could fly no faster than a plump pelican. The carrier sagged from the weight of Tutupia's gifts, and the wind was against them.

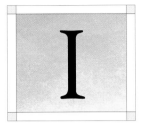N FAIRY HAVEN, the water was an inch deep, up to the knees of the fairies. In the dells and dingles it was an inch and a half deep. This may not seem serious, but if a fairy fell out of the air, her wings would become waterlogged and she would have to struggle to stand up. Fairies have drowned in puddles.

Two dozen water talents were keeping the Home Tree dry, for now. A squad of mud talents was building a dike around it. They held their wings high, their shoulders aching.

Beyond the dike, artist Bess had spread out a canvas on which she'd painted a desert scene so convincing that the ground under it stayed dry. Nearby, a squad of cooking talents used fairy dust to boil the floodwater as soon as it bubbled up. Most of it evaporated, creating a thick fog.

But these successes were limited. Most of Fairy Haven was wet.

The animal talents had saved as many earthworms as they could, but fewer and fewer of the creatures were reaching the surface. Beck was rounding up the moles and leading them to safety.

While the fairies worked, their thoughts were with the questers, wondering if a wand was on the way. Everyone tried to think of an excuse to borrow it before it descended into the lagoon forever.

Vidia, cooped up in Rani's room, was being driven wild by Rani's leaky ceiling. She was about to stuff Rani's pet minnow into the leak—when she had a better idea. She flew to the ceiling and used the thumbtack heel of her left shoe to enlarge the pinprick hole. Plaster chips fell into Minnie's tub.

Prilla had been helping Dulcie bake vast sheets of sponge cake to mop up floodwater, when it occurred to her that her own talent might end the flood. She pictured the imaginary tunnel that took her to the mainland. She blinked through it and flew above the heads of Clumsy children at a puppet show, calling out to them, "Clap to make the flood dry up in Fairy Haven!"

Most looked up and clapped.

She blinked to the rehearsal of a school play. "Clap to end the fairies' flood!"

The young actors clapped.

She blinked to four children playing Go Fish. "Clap to lower the water in Fairy Haven!"

The four clapped.

Prilla returned to Fairy Haven. The water had risen another

quarter inch. But maybe without her it would have risen a half inch. She blinked away again.

Mother Dove was alone. Beck had brought lunch, but then had to return to the moles. Mother Dove longed to fly to the questers, keep them on course, remind them that effort was better than wishes. But she couldn't leave the egg unless her own wish came true. The egg needed the warmth of her body. She could leave a chick for a while but not an egg.

The wind was so strong that Ree and Tink made almost no headway against it.

Rani noticed neither the wind nor the sag of the carrier. She saw only the wand at her feet. She bent down for it.

"Rani!"

Rani dropped the wand guiltily and turned.

Tink was flying backward, her ponytail blown against her right cheek. "Rani, wish for new wings so you can help us."

Rani wanted new wings. She missed flying and hated having to depend on Brother Dove or other fairies to take her everywhere. But she wanted friendship with Soop more than she wanted wings.

She saw how low the carrier was flying. "I'll throw Queen

Tutupia's presents over." She jettisoned them all, except the picnic basket, which weighed little.

The carrier bobbed higher, but they gained almost no speed.

"Rani," Tink said, "we need another pair of—"

"—wings. The wind will die down soon."

Tink didn't even tug her bangs. She just looked disgusted and turned to fly forward again.

Consumed by wand madness, Rani didn't care. She reached for the wand.

"Rani!"

Hugging the wand defiantly, Rani faced Ree.

"I command . . ." Ree touched her tiara. She hardly ever issued commands. There were better ways to rule. "I command you to wish for new—"

"—wings. I won't." Rani had never disobeyed Ree before. "Why don't you wish for them for me? You can wish it as easily as I can."

Ree didn't want to give her wish to Rani so Rani could have whatever she wanted and wings, too. Tink didn't either and was furious—at herself for not being generous and at Rani for being selfish.

With as much dignity as she could muster, Ree said, "I'll discuss your contrariness . . ." She didn't want to call it more than that. ". . . later."

Rani closed her eyes and thought, Make Soop think of me as her friend. Make her like me. Make her like me very much. She waved the wand.

As had become her custom, Soop was in a tower room of the mermaids' castle, scanning the sea for a tiny fairy with a wand. Abruptly, she found herself regretting her harsh words to the fairy. And she'd yelled at her. That had certainly been a mistake. Rani might be a fairy, but she was a superior one, worthy of a mermaid's friendship.

Soop wondered if she should stop flooding Fairy Haven. It wasn't polite to drown your friend's home.

But her anger was stronger than her goodwill. The flood was on until the wand was delivered. Mermaids weren't to be trifled with.

However, if Rani did return, Soop would give her a warm welcome.

Rani put down the wand, satisfied. She breathed deeply. My first breath, she thought, as a mermaid's friend. She didn't feel different, but she knew she was different. She brushed away a tear— and remembered her argument with Tink and Ree.

Now she recognized how slowly they were moving. At this rate it would take a month just to reach the sea, and their fairy dust would run out long before then. Ahead of her, she saw the strain in Tink's shoulders. She saw Ree kick the air fruitlessly.

I should have wished for wings, she thought.

She still could.

Wand madness crept back in. She thought Mother Dove might approve of this second wish, since it was to help end the flood.

She raised the wand. She'd never before broken a promise to Mother Dove.

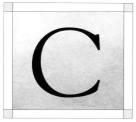LUMSY HOUSES, farms, factories, and roads passed beneath the carrier at a maddeningly slow rate.

Give me wings that can fly through the air and swim in the water. Rani had a new thought. Make me able to breathe and speak in both air and water. She waved the wand.

Was that three wishes? she wondered. Did I break my promise twice?

Ah. She wept glad tears as she joined Tink and Ree at the carrier cord. Flying was as wonderful as weeping!

Mother Dove felt Rani's extra wishes, although she didn't know what they were. Impetuous Rani, she thought. The first promise breaker.

"Clap to dry up the flood!" Prilla flew down the aisle of a school bus. She heard clapping as she blinked away.

She landed on the shoulder of a Clumsy woman who stood at a window next to a Clumsy man. Prilla looked around the

room. They were in a child's bedroom, but there was no child.

How odd. Prilla had never arrived in a place without a child. There was no point to it. Adult Clumsies couldn't see or hear her.

She was about to blink away, but before she did, she saw, through the open window, a Clumsy girl sitting motionless on a swing in the backyard.

"Why doesn't she swing?" the woman said. "Why doesn't she play? Why is it she never laughs?"

Prilla thought there was something familiar about the girl.

The man said, "Dr. Barry says there's nothing wrong with Sara."

Sara? Prilla thought. The name was familiar, too, although it wasn't a fairy name. She flew outside. "Clap to end the flood."

Her face dull, Sara raised her hands to clap. Then she saw Prilla. She clapped wildly and laughed and began to swing and clap at the same time.

Prilla felt a quiver in her chest. She landed in the child's lap and wondered why she felt as cozy there as she did snuggled in Mother Dove's feathers.

The girl must have been her laugher! Sara Quirtle was her name. A baby's first laugh flits away from the baby and turns into a fairy. Usually the two don't encounter each other again.

As Sara Quirtle swung and laughed, Prilla looked at the

house. In the window, she saw Sara Quirtle's parents watching and laughing, too. They hugged.

Sara Quirtle sang, "You're back. You're back. Welcome back. I'm glad you're back." She pumped her legs extra hard.

But Prilla couldn't stay! Never Land needed her. Besides, she didn't know how to stay.

She jumped up. She did three midair handstands and another cartwheel. "I have to go. Farewell, Sara Quirtle." She flew over the roof. When she was too small for Sara Quirtle to see, she turned.

The swing was slowing. Sara Quirtle was no longer pumping, and her face was as slack as it had been when Prilla first saw it.

Prilla's glow flickered and almost went out. Oh, no! Sara Quirtle must be incomplete!

Occasionally, a fairy arrives in Never Land incomplete, because a bit came off during the ocean journey to the island. The scout Russell, for example, who wished to be Mother Dove's favorite, was incomplete. Mother Dove loved the incompletes as completely as she loved every other fairy. Still, incompleteness set one apart.

Prilla had never heard of an incomplete Clumsy. She feared she might have Sara Quirtle's missing part.

She was correct. Sara Quirtle's first laugh had been so explosive that a snippet of Sara Quirtle had lodged in Prilla and been absorbed. It was the Sara Quirtle in Prilla that gave Prilla her clapping talent and her talent for blinking over to the mainland.

Prilla took two wing flaps back toward Sara Quirtle and stopped, Never Land tugging at her. She wanted to stay longer, but—

The flood had risen. Feeling hopeless, Prilla blinked to a mainland schoolyard. "Clap to help Fairy Haven!"

She saw a dot in the sky above her. Her wings quivered. A hawk?

Wrong shape for a hawk. She squinted.

The balloon carrier! There it was, and now she had a wish.

As she flew upward, Prilla wondered if Mother Dove would disapprove of her using the wand since she wasn't a quester.

She drew closer and saw three fairies at the cord. Rani had wings again!

Nobody was in the carrier. Prilla could wave the wand, and Mother Dove wouldn't have to find out.

The wand was smaller than Prilla expected—shiny and jaunty, its squiggle catching the afternoon sun. It would be easy to wave. Prilla picked it up without landing. The questers didn't turn around.

In a rush, she whispered, "Without taking anything away from me or my talent, make Sara Quirtle complete." She waved the wand, then replaced it carefully.

Completing someone was complicated. The wand had to think to obey. A wide-awake spark flared in its sleeping mind. It granted Prilla's wish, then returned to deep slumber.

Prilla flew with all her might to reach Ree and Rani and Tink and help them pull the carrier. As she drew close, she got her first clear view of Rani's wings.

If fish could fly they'd have wings like hers, webbed and covered with oily scales. Prilla was easy to please, but those wings were unsightly!

Prilla grabbed the carrier cord and started pulling, too. "Hello!"

They didn't hear her over the wind. She shouted, "Hello!"

They heard and knew it was Prilla without turning their heads. No one except Prilla said hello.

"I'll fly with you as long as I can."

With Prilla pulling, too, the carrier made better progress. Ree thought she saw the sea in the distance.

"How high is the flood?" Ree shouted.

"Four inches."

Up to a fairy's shoulders!

Tink's smile vanished. "Has anyone—"

"—drowned?"

But Prilla was gone. Her *good-bye* lingered in the wind.

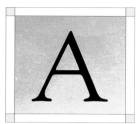

AS SOON AS Prilla arrived in Fairy Haven she blinked away again. There was Sara Quirtle, on the floor of a living room with another girl. The two were coloring on the same page of an enormous pad. Sara Quirtle was biting her lip in concentration and pressing her crayon into the paper so hard it broke.

Prilla celebrated Sara Quirtle's completion by turning an aerial cartwheel.

The girls were drawing fairies. The other girl's fairy was huge, covering most of her side of the page. Sara Quirtle's was fist-sized and upside down, doing a handstand.

Prilla swooped onto the pad. She landed on her hands, imitating her image.

Sara Quirtle laughed. "My fairy!"

"Clap to end the flood!" Prilla blinked away.

Rani knew Tink had been pleased with her ever since she'd wished for new wings, and Tink's approval made her feel doubly guilty. She blurted out, "I made two wishes."

Tink yelled, "What?"

Rani shouted, "I broke . . ."

The wind died.

". . . my promise." The words were almost loud enough to be heard in Never Land. "I made two wishes."

Tink and Ree were stunned. They hadn't considered breaking their promises to Mother Dove. Now the possibility bloomed in each of them.

"You both hate me!" Rani wailed.

"I don't hate you," Tink said. "I'm glad you wished for wings. Now we know the wand works, and you're fixed." More or less. She thought the new wings would look better on a lizard.

"I don't hate you, either," Ree said. "You were right to listen to me."

Tink asked, "What was your other—"

"—wish?" Rani's glow turned pink. "To make Soop be my friend."

Tink thought it a wasted wish. She didn't know what she wanted to wish for, although images of Peter Pan kept popping into her mind. Ree thought about wanding up new laughs for Fairy Haven.

An hour passed. Two hours. They reached the open sea. Tink squinted at the horizon. Never Land could move about the ocean. It could be nearby, looking for them.

But the horizon was flat.

Good, she thought. I have more time to think.

That's how wand-mad she was. She'd forgotten the flood.

She decided to touch the wand. She let go of the balloon-carrier cord.

Surprised, Rani tried to pull for both of them. Ree turned to watch Tink.

The carrier lurched when Tink landed, then steadied. She sprinkled fairy dust on the wand and stroked it. The glow in her hand grew brighter. The wand *was* a kind of pot, maybe a stew pot for cooking up wishes. "Are you dreaming?" she murmured. Her fingers tingled. Yes, it was dreaming.

She picked it up. She hadn't planned her wish. She hadn't

meant to wish anything yet. The wish simply tumbled out. "Make Peter Pan fall in love with a clamshell, an ordinary clamshell." She waved the wand and put it down.

"Tink!" Rani cried.

Tink met Rani's eye. "He deserves it." She returned to the carrier cord. Her heart was racing, and she fought back tears. She would not cry again over Peter.

Instead, she grinned. Peter in love with a clamshell.

On Marooners' Rock, Peter was regaling a dozen mermaids with a tale he'd learned from Wendy. He said, "The little mermaid wished to marry the handsome prince."

The mermaids hooted with laughter. A real mermaid would never fall in love with a Clumsy!

"She longed—" He broke off, feeling an urge to walk on the beach and look for shells. He dived off the rock.

The fairy-dust talents were in the mill, rubbing beeswax on the pumpkin canisters that held the year's supply of fairy dust. The beeswax would keep the canisters dry for a while. However, as soon as water got through, the dust inside would be ruined.

Terence thought his arm was going to fall off, but he continued rubbing. Then, suddenly, he began to tremble. Overwork, he thought.

No, not overwork. Tink. She was in trouble! He felt it in his glow. He dropped his geranium-leaf rubbing cloth and flew out of the mill. Three fairies called to him, but he didn't answer.

He flew to the shore and set out toward the mainland. He didn't think about food or fairy dust for the journey. He didn't think about the immensity of the ocean and the tininess of three fairies and a balloon carrier. He thought only of Tink.

Vidia broke through Rani's ceiling and flew out the window of the room above, shouting, "Catch me!"

The scouts didn't try. Not a fairy alive could catch Vidia. A scout headed for the nest to tell Mother Dove.

Vidia flew out to sea. Unlike Terence, she had plenty of fairy dust. One way or another, she always did.

Night fell. The wind changed and blew at their backs. The questers made rapid progress.

Ree began to think of herself as Queen Clarion the Great because of the magnificent wish she would make. The possibilities swirled in her head: more laughs, an improved Home Tree, a museum, domesticated tortoises. Her tiara blew off, and she didn't even notice.

Rani kept thinking she saw the island twinkling on the horizon. But it never was.

ELEVEN

T MIDNIGHT, Temma, a shoemaking-talent fairy, drowned. Her last thought was that she'd never get her wand wish—to make a shoe with a toe that flickered back and forth from pointy to round.

Beck went to tell Mother Dove, who already knew. They wept together.

"Could the wand bring Temma back?" Beck asked.

"No. Not even a wand can do that."

Terence flew through the night. He wished fairy glows were brighter. The questers might not be far away. A dozen yards off and he wouldn't see them. He could fly until his dust gave out, and they might already be behind him.

If I die, he thought, it will be for love.

Dawn came. Rani opened the picnic basket. Nestled inside were lentil sandwiches, sesame-seed chips, and cherry tartlets. She took a sandwich. Another appeared. "It's a magic basket!"

The morning passed. Every few minutes, Tink closed her eyes and counted to a hundred, hoping that when she opened them she'd see Never Land.

Ree evaluated wand project after wand project. She was debating raising a mountain under Fairy Haven when Rani said, "If I threw the wand overboard, I think Never Land would appear in two minutes."

"Don't!" Ree said. "I forbid it."

"Rani wouldn't," Tink said. "Fairy Haven would—"

"—be done for. Ree, you know I wouldn't."

Ree nodded, feeling strange. For a moment she thought she might have wand madness. But she couldn't. She'd spent a day with the wand and hadn't used it yet.

Tink, who was convinced of Ree's madness, flew back to the wand and waved it, unaware that she was breaking her one-wish promise. "Cure Queen Ree of wand madness. Cure us all."

Another thing a wand can't do is cure wand madness. It can only cause the disease.

Terence estimated that he had an hour's supply of fairy dust left, including the dust that was clinging to his frock coat and the days-old dust in the toes of his socks.

He shook his hair and his sleeves, creating a mist of dust. He imagined Tink scowling, Tink dimpling, Tink tugging her bangs,

Tink sticking out the tip of her tongue as she worked.

What was that distant glimmer? Tink? The questers? He put on a burst of speed, the last burst he had left. Even so, he thought the glimmer too far off to reach.

Ree considered hawks. Beck always maintained they were dignified and honorable. But how honorable was it to eat a fairy?

What if she waved the wand and shrank them? She wouldn't change anything else about them. They could go on being dignified and honorable.

She flew onto the carrier. "Wand, I command you to shrink the hawks of Never Land to a quarter of an inch from beak to tail." She picked up the wand and waved it. Perhaps she should change her title from queen to empress. Her true reign had just begun.

Beck heard the hawks' cry. Every animal talent heard it, a surprised squawk followed by a woebegone call, strong and deep at first, then weak and high as the birds shrank.

Beck flew out of her animal-rescue boat. She flicked fairy dust into the air and blew on it. Then she headed for Mother Dove. A hawk would meet her there.

The golden hawk arrived a few minutes after Beck. He was

the oldest hawk, the magical one, whose feathers were brown on top and pure gold underneath.

Beck's glow winked out when she saw him. He was tiny! "Someone used the wand, right?" she said to Mother Dove. Her glow returned, deepening to a furious purple.

"Yes, dear." Mother Dove ached for the hawks. She was convinced Ree had made the wish.

"Who?" Beck asked.

"It doesn't matter."

Beck knew Mother Dove would never tell. "How could they have done anything to the golden hawk?" He'd helped save Never Land after the hurricane.

He landed on Beck's head. Hawks aren't complainers, and they're not chatty. He didn't say there was no joy without hunting. He didn't say the fairies might as well have killed all the hawks. He only said, "How will we feed ourselves?"

"We'll help," Beck promised. The animal talents could feed them, but food wasn't enough. Fairies couldn't give them back their pride.

"Mother Dove? What can we do?"

Mother Dove was silent. They couldn't do anything.

Terence made out Tink even before he saw the balloon carrier. He was flying slowly now, using muscle mostly and hardly any dust. His breath was coming in gasps, and she was much too far away to hear, but he called anyway, "Tink!"

At least he'd seen her one more time.

She saw his glow. "What's that?" She pointed. "A firefly?"

"It's not a hawk," Ree said. "We're safe from them."

Rani spit and shaped the drop of water into a lens. "It's Terence!" She observed him for a moment. "He's dropping! He'll go under."

That was when they should have used the wand. A single wave, and Terence would have been in the balloon carrier.

But none of them thought of it. Instead, they swooped down, leaving the carrier with the wand hovering above.

They'd almost reached him when the water closed over his head.

Rani dived in and caught him just before his breath ran out. If not for her new wings, she wouldn't have had the strength to pull him to the surface. Everyone was puffing by the time they'd hoisted him into the carrier.

"You're safe!" he gasped out to Tink, smiling at her.

She tugged her bangs. "Of course, I'm safe. We saved—"

"—you!" Rani started laughing.

Tink dimpled. Ree smiled.

Rani flew out of the carrier to shake herself pleasantly damp.

Ree checked around, beginning to frown. Tink stood over Terence, making sure he was all right. He thought he could look at her forever. Then he realized—he'd been in the water, and he was alive! He saw Rani flapping her wings.

"New wings, and they swim!" he said.

Ree pushed the picnic basket aside.

Rani nodded, looking both proud and distressed, thinking of Mother Dove. "And I can breathe underwater. I could have—"

"Where's the wand?" Ree said. Her voice rose. "Where's the wand?"

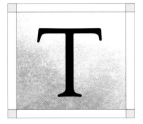HEY THOUGHT the wand had fallen out of the carrier when they'd gone for Terence. Rani dived into the sea and spent half an hour looking for it without success.

There was nothing to do but turn the carrier back toward the mainland. Rani wondered if Tutupia would make them all disappear when she found out they'd lost a wand. Terence checked their supply of fairy dust. He doubted they had enough to go to the castle and then reach home.

Ree discovered her tiara was missing, too. She almost felt worse about it than about the wand. It was as though half her head had come off, or as if she no longer had a name.

One more thing was gone: wand madness.

At first they were too taken up with the lost wand to notice the change in themselves. But soon Tink remembered what she'd done to Peter. It was meaner than putting a dent in a pot on purpose, and a permanent dent at that.

Rani was still glad Soop was her friend, and she was still thrilled to fly again, but she felt with renewed force how disappointed in her Mother Dove was going to be. Ree wondered how she could have shrunk the hawks. What if they were all dead? What if everything inside them hadn't fit into a quarter of an inch and they'd burst? And she'd wanted to be empress! She'd deserved to lose her tiara.

"If Tutupia gives us another wand," Ree said, "let's ask her to lock it in a box that only a mermaid can—"

"—open." Rani wondered what a mermaid with wand madness would do.

After that, everyone quizzed Terence about the flood, but he'd been at the mill the whole time and had little information for them.

They pulled him in the balloon carrier until his wings dried. Then he sprinkled himself with fairy dust and joined them at the cord.

After that they should have made good progress, with four fairies pulling, but the wind was against them again.

Mother Dove's nest was only nine inches above the water. Beck and Prilla and twelve more fairies came to move it to a higher branch. While they were airborne, Mother Dove cooed, "We're going up, my love. Up!" Her voice caught. "You're flying, dear."

This was the closest her egg would ever come to flight.

Naturally, Vidia had the wand. She'd arrived while the questers were saving Terence. She'd viewed the unguarded carrier as a stroke of luck and hadn't cared why.

Waving the wand, she'd said, "Wand, sweetheart, make me able to fly as fast as I want, as far as I want, as long as I want."

Of course, she should have put the wand back, but she held on to it in case she needed to adjust her wish.

She felt a surge of strength in her shoulder blades. She began to fly and was easily able to achieve her ordinary top speed, then faster, smoothly faster.

Far above, a petrel crossed a cloud.

Catch it!

The bird squawked as she flashed by. She laughed at its surprise.

Faster!

The air stung her face and roared in her ears. This was what she'd always dreamed of.

Faster!

She raced toward the setting sun. Her ears smarted. She touched one and looked at her hand. Blood on her fingers.

Didn't matter.

Faster!

There was the mainland. So soon. She zoomed over lakes,

cities, deserts, mountains, canyons, plains, and back over the open sea.

Faster!

As she flew, she stroked the wand. "Dear wand. Sweet wand. Kind wand."

She circled the world—three times. The sun rose and set thrice, although to the questers only half an hour had crawled by.

Vidia wasn't breathing hard. Her lungs weren't threatening to explode. Her heart wasn't about to burst from her chest. This was heaven. She flew straight up toward the transparent daytime moon. When her hair and lips froze, she turned and dived back to earth.

There was nothing to it. She could fly infinitely fast. Infinitely! And there'd still be nothing to it.

The elation drained out of her. The strain of trying to fly faster was gone now, but so was the triumph of beating her own record, of eking another scintilla of speed out of her tired wings.

This effortless speed was boring.

She hovered in the midst of a high cloud. "I'm grateful, love," she told the wand. "But now I need my old flying back. Wand, darling, make me fly as I used to, before my first command." She waved it.

She felt no change. She flew and found there had been no change.

Maybe she'd phrased her wish incorrectly. "Dear Wand, I command you to make me fly no faster than the natural strength of my wings and my talent and fairy dust let me." She waved it.

Nothing changed.

Vidia thought she might not be waving the wand hard enough. She waved it harder and longer.

Nothing changed.

"Wand, cutie pie, make me earn my speed."

It wriggled, deep in a wandish dream.

What did the wriggle mean? "Are you listening, Wand?" She shook it. If it had had a neck, she would have strangled it.

She tried yet another wording. And another. And another.

She tried flicking the wand, flipping it, flapping it, wagging it, jiggling it.

She screamed. She wept.

Through the night she tried to reverse her wish. Her fairy dust ran out, but she no longer needed fairy dust to fly.

At dawn she admitted defeat.

She remembered Mother Dove's warning—that her wish would break her heart.

THIRTEEN

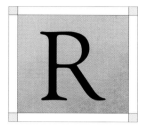

REE CALCULATED that they'd left Fairy Haven four days ago. It would be a miracle if a dozen fairies hadn't drowned by now.

Rani thought about what would happen if they returned without a wand. Everyone would have to find a new home. They might have to emigrate to the mainland.

"Ree, darling . . ." Vidia flew backwards in front of the four fairies, holding the wand.

They lunged at her, but she sped off, so fast that they knew what her wish had been.

Wand madness returned.

"Dearheart . . . Queen Ree . . . Queen Clarion . . ." Vidia hovered a foot away. "Tell me how to reverse my command."

"Give me the wand," Ree said sternly.

"First tell me, sweet."

"When Rani dives with the wand, I'll tell you."

"Now, or no wand."

Ree shook her head.

"Tink, love, you tell me. I need to fix myself."

Tink said nothing.

"Rani—"

"—honey. I won't tell you."

"Ree, sugarplum, if the wand goes to Soop, can I still reverse my wish?"

Ree had never before lied to a subject. "Yes."

Vidia gave her the wand. "If you lied, Your Majesty, love, I'll haul you to the sun and throw you in."

The fairies turned the carrier. Vidia joined them at the cord, and the five began to fly. But the questers and Terence could

only cling to the cord in terror while Vidia zoomed along. When they were halfway across the sea, she heard their shouts. She stopped while they flew into the carrier.

Then she pulled them all, flying so fast the air felt like knives against their faces.

Vidia flew around the globe and over the mainland. She set off across the sea in a new direction.

Tink was imagining new kinds of pots—pots that could cook away from the stove, frying pans that wouldn't need oil, pots that would know when food was cooked. Ree was thinking of bringing the Giant Shimmering fairies to Fairy Haven to work for the Never fairies. Rani thought of turning herself into a dolphin for a day.

Terence looked from Tink to the wand in Ree's lap. Soon they'd be in Never Land. The wand would be lost to him forever, and with it his chance to have Tink's love. He leaned forward, as if he were going to speak to Ree, and in a graceful, gentle gesture, took the wand. "Make Tink . . ."

She turned to him, startled.

". . . like me, like me . . . romantically." He waved the wand.

For a split second, Tink thought of Peter and his clamshell. She raised her hand to pull her bangs, but her hand stopped, and she smiled at Terence.

Terence saw her change her mind, go from the irritation

she really felt to the happiness she had to feel. He didn't know whether to be glad or sad. Tink liked him. But was she still Tink?

Vidia slowed to the speed of an ordinary fast flier. "Loves, I can't find Never Land."

"It doesn't want the wand," Ree said.

Tink wondered if she'd ever see her pots again. "I'm glad you're here," she told Terence.

"I'm glad, too." He added, "We haven't tried fairy dust." He took a handful of dust out of the sack. "Look through it as I go." He flew around the carrier, trailing a stream of dust.

The others squinted into it, hoping to see the island on the horizon. They didn't, although they did glimpse a spire of Tutupia's castle on the mainland.

"I'll dive into the water with the wand," Rani said. "Maybe Never Land will think it's gone. I'll stay under for half an hour."

"Dearheart, you think Never Land will simply—"

"—appear? Maybe."

No one could think of anything better to try. Rani took the wand.

"Don't lose it, sweet—"

"—heart. I won't."

Tink would have told her to take care, but she was smiling into Terence's brown eyes.

Rani dived.

Vidia rose high above the balloon carrier to catch the first sight of Never Land.

Ree felt her mind clear. It was easier to think with the wand underwater. She said, "I wanted to enslave the Shimmerers."

Tink felt the madness lift, too. "I broke Peter, and I'm broken." She tucked her arm through Terence's. "But I don't want to be mended."

Terence found the courage to touch Tink's ponytail, which was exactly as soft and springy as he'd imagined.

"I wish I could unshrink the hawks," Ree said.

Tink remembered her ideas for new pots. Pots were perfect just as they were. "I don't want to make more wishes."

Ree said, "If the wand were awake—"

"It's asleep?" Terence said.

Ree nodded. "If it were awake, we'd be safe."

"Why?" Terence asked.

"Because it wouldn't obey us," Tink said. "We could make wishes, and it wouldn't listen. And if we could make it obey, we could make it reverse our mistakes."

Luckily, Vidia was too far off to hear this.

"So wake it up." Terence thought Tink could do anything.

Tink wondered if she could. She'd been able to feel its sleep.

"But," Ree told him, "Tutupia said it could do things to us

if it were awake. She said it might be mischievous. And some wands don't have kind hearts."

"Tink can tame it and fix its heart. Then it will be safe for Soop."

"It's not safe now," Ree said.

Tink tugged gently at Terence's ear. "I'm not a Great Wandy." But it would be the most thrilling thing to try.

Ree said, "You could make it reverse our wishes."

"Except Terence's," Tink said.

He said nothing, feeling torn in two.

Ree said, "Mother Dove would want every wish reversed, if the wand were awake."

They knew that was true.

"Then I'd reverse Terence's," Tink said. "It wouldn't make any difference. I'd feel the same."

He knew she wouldn't. She hadn't cared about him before. Now she'd hate him for meddling with her feelings.

"Tink, try when Rani comes back," Ree said. "Then maybe Never Land really will come."

Underwater, Rani swam in a circle, holding the wand, mad as ever. A school of herring passed a few yards away. Below her, she saw an orange sea fan, as big and full of branches as an apple tree.

She could stay in the water now endlessly. She could create a race of water fairies. They could live in this very sea fan, practicing their talents and being snobby about mermaids.

But they wouldn't have Mother Dove. Rani knew she couldn't wand up an underwater Mother Dove.

Oh! A shark! Using her talent, Rani made the water around her solid. The shark would bump its nose if it came close.

But it barreled by.

Rani treaded water, feeling silly for hiding to fool Never Land. Never Land had never been fooled before.

What if she didn't try to fool it? What if she really gave up the wand? She could summon Soop and make sure they were friends. Rani could leave the wand with her. Then Never Land would appear and let its fairies in.

"Bring . . ." She hesitated. Before she gave the wand away, she could make Fairy Haven safe forever. No more hurricanes. No more floods. No more risk to Mother Dove or to any of them. No more disasters. No more anger. No more sadness. Only happy fairies working happily on their talents. Only happy Mother Dove, cooing happily.

She raised the wand.

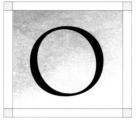

ON HER NEW branch, Mother Dove sensed Rani's wish. No! No! That's the worst wish! She cooed and tried to send the coos across the island and into the ocean's depths. Rani, don't make it.

Rani remembered how much she loved to cry, not only happy tears but sad ones, too. She chose not to make the wish. Instead, she said, "Bring Soop to me. Don't hurt her." She waved the wand.

It obeyed, and Never Land decided to come with Soop.

At first Rani felt no change. A speckled jellyfish drifted by, waggling its frilly mouth arms. Rani was about to repeat her wish when she felt the currents strengthen.

Above the sea, the fairies saw an enormous wave form in the distance. The wind blew up. The fairies fought to stay above the spot where Rani had dived, although they were no longer sure precisely where that was.

As the wave approached, it began to curl. A whirlpool formed. Tink thought she saw Rani spinning in the vortex, clutching the wand. She squeezed Terence's hand so hard he winced.

Then the sea closed over the whirlpool, and the sea's surface became as flat as a pond. Ree and Tink and Terence stared into it, hoping to see Rani rising toward them.

Vidia flew down to the balloon carrier and said, "My sweeties, look what's come."

Underwater, Rani whipped round and round, with no more control than a shred of seaweed, her arms, legs, and new wings spread flat against a wall of water. The whirlpool drew more and more of the ocean into its orbit. Rani saw a manatee, a herd of whales, a sunken ship with twelve masts. . . .

Oh! There was the mermaids' castle, with dozens of mermaids clinging to the girders.

The whirlpool slowed. The castle settled on the ocean floor, and there was Soop in a tower room, her long pink scarf candy-striped around her.

The water stilled. Rani held the wand in front of her. She swam toward Soop, her wings sweeping the water like fins.

Soop unwound her scarf. Where was she? She looked around. Home! Home? How could she be home when she'd been flung through the ocean?

"Soop!" Rani cried. "Here's the wand."

Soop saw Rani. The fairy she liked so much had brought the wand! And the fairy had wings again. Soop smiled her best smile and waved her scarf. She sent her thoughts to Fairy Haven. In less time than it takes to think a single word, she dried up the flood.

Ree reached up for her tiara, then remembered it wasn't there. Tink, who had never clung to anyone before, clung to Terence. Vidia said, "Home, sweet home, darlings."

They were hovering a few yards from Marooners' Rock.

Soop and Rani swam toward each other. Just before they met, Rani had a last mad thought of waving the wand and wishing herself far away.

Soop took it.

"Can we swim together?" Rani said.

"Certainly."

Mermaids aren't curious about other creatures. Soop didn't wonder how Rani could speak and breathe underwater, or why she now had wings.

The two circled the castle together. Rani imitated Soop's elegant breaststroke. She held her legs together and swished them, as Soop was swishing her tail. She dared to think she might be nearly as graceful as a mermaid.

They passed a room where a mermaid was counting out cockleshell coins. In another room, a merman polished a sculpture made of coral. A clutch of merchildren were led through the shell museum.

Soop whirled in the water and swam backward in front of Rani. "My friend! I haven't welcomed you. Mermaids always welcome their friends."

Rani didn't know what the welcome would be. She had never been happier. Her glow burned so bright that the water around her simmered.

Holding the wand to her heart, Soop began her favorite ballad, one she usually sang on moonless nights when the clouds hung low. It told the tragic tale of a mermaid who loses her nautilus shell to an evil octopus.

A mermaid's voice is undiminished by water. Soop's song rang out as clearly as it would have if she'd been singing on Marooners' Rock at midnight.

Oh, no! Rani wanted to beg Soop to stop singing, but before her mouth had opened halfway, the song had her in its thrall.

Soop sang in Mermish, a liquid language without consonants. For a moment Rani thought she understood anyway. The song was so beautiful, its melancholy so poignant.

Rani's transformation began. She fought it. Through rising pain and panic, she tried to remain a fairy, to hold on to her fairy shape and her talent for water. When she knew she was losing the battle, she tried to call out, to tell Soop that wand wishes were permanent, but she couldn't do that either. Soop's voice was too compelling.

A bat's mind began to take over, and the song seemed to change. The joy and despair leached out of it, because bats are logical and pay little attention to feeling.

Rani didn't look very different yet, although her body was shrinking and her hands were growing, and webs were forming between her fingers. Her bat's mind wondered what she was doing underwater.

While Soop continued to sing, Rani started to swim toward the surface. Soop, who knew nothing of fairies turning into bats, was surprised and hurt, but, engrossed in her song, she went on singing. Perhaps if she'd stopped, the process unfolding in Rani might have reversed itself. It might not have been too late.

Soop didn't stop. Rani-bat kicked hard and rose above the castle. The strains of Soop's song followed her through the lagoon.

Tink saw a figure rise out of the water. "Look!"

Rani's dress was draped around the bat, the side seams ripped to accommodate the bat's wings. A leafkerchief wafted down to the sea.

Rani-bat's vision was worse than poor, and the daylight

almost blinded her. Still, the shore looked more appealing than the sea, so that was the way she went.

Was any vestige of pure Rani left? Yes, more than a vestige. Rani was crammed into a pinprick in Rani-bat's brain. Rani could think—anguished thoughts. She could feel—terror and rage. She could hear through Rani-bat's ears, peer through Rani-bat's weak eyes, but she couldn't make Rani-bat's body do anything. As Rani-bat's wings beat across the water, Rani tried to cry for help, in case Tink and the others were there.

She couldn't make a single word come out.

FIFTEEN

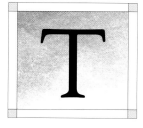 INK AND TERENCE took off after the bat. Ree started to go, too, but Vidia caught her arm.

"How do I reverse my wish, love?"

Ree tried to shake free of Vidia's grip. "Get Rani!"

"How do I reverse my wish?"

"Catch Rani!"

"Sweetheart, tell me first." She let go of Ree.

Ree stood straight in the air, as regal as she could be without her tiara. "You can't reverse it."

Vidia's glow turned bright red. "You lied."

Ree fluttered backward. "The wand can't reverse wishes. It's asleep. Only an awake wand—"

"Why didn't you wake it?"

"We were going—"

Vidia was gone. She was circling the earth, a red comet, a dying star, until finally she landed in her own sour-plum tree. She entered her room and stretched out on her bed. She had no desire ever to fly again.

Tink and Terence lost sight of Rani-bat in the brush at the edge of the beach.

Underwater, Soop finished her song. She wondered if she'd sung badly or if her new friend was angry with her. She hoped Rani would return soon so she could find out. Perhaps they could sing together then.

In the meantime, she had a wand.

Rani-bat flew toward the Wough River. From inside the bat, Rani tried to blow herself up into a fairy again.

Halfway to the river, Rani-bat found a decaying cherry tree that was home to a colony of bats. From the edge of a tree hole she cheeped, "Pardon me. So sorry to be a bother. I should have made an appointment. I should have a letter of introduction. But I had no advance warning of my need for a residence. Would—"

Rani tried to make the bat stop talking. Fairies didn't say "pardon me" or "sorry." And Rani didn't want to have anything to do with those bats—or with the bat encasing her.

Rani-bat felt something gnawing at a corner of her mind. She ignored the feeling and kept speaking. "—you be so kind? Might I ask . . ."

Eighty-seven bats shifted to make room for the newcomer.

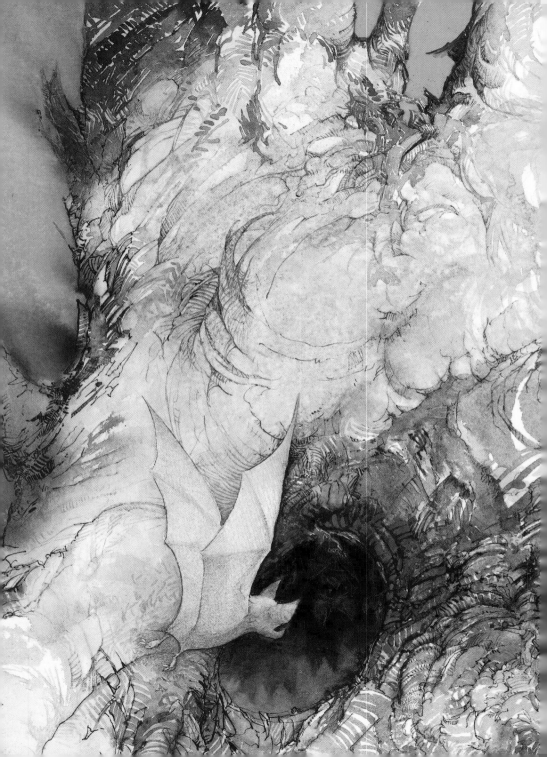

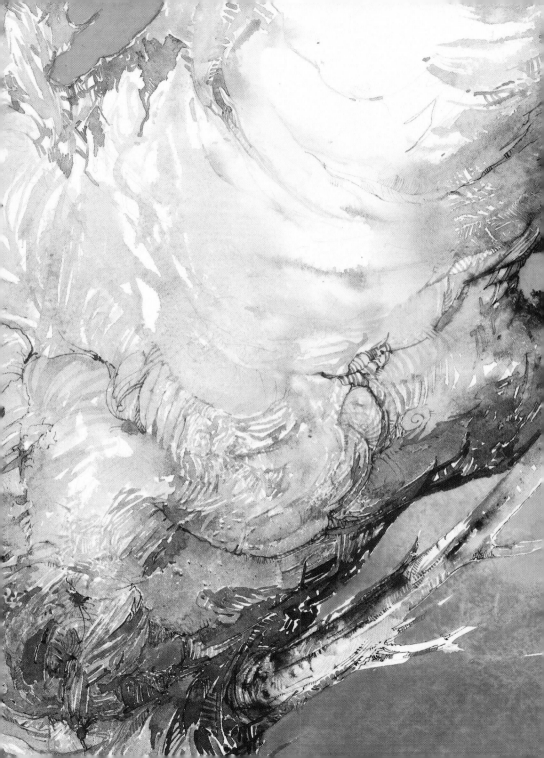

Rani-bat flew in. She settled next to another bat, right up against her, fur-to-fur.

Ugh! Rani wanted to scratch herself all over. She wanted to sneeze a big, wet sneeze.

Rani-bat wrapped her wings around herself for warmth.

Rani was roasting, and she couldn't even sweat.

Rani-bat fell asleep instantly.

Rani was wide awake. She was miserable. She'd probably be a bat forever. She'd never use her talent again. She couldn't cry. She couldn't even make her nose run.

She'd delivered the wand, but she hadn't warned Soop that her wishes couldn't be undone. Soop might already have wished something she didn't mean.

There is little privacy in the mermaids' castle, where the rooms, except for the wind room, have no walls. Soop went to her bedroom and entered her "concealment forest." A concealment forest is a grove of tall seaweed that shields a mermaid from prying eyes.

In her forest, Soop took out the wand. She wondered how much she needed to tell it and how much it understood without being told. She began. "Sir Wand, this command concerns my friend Pah."

Soop and Pah often quarreled, but in the past they'd always

made up. However, their latest squabble, about a song title, had taken place more than a month ago. Neither had spoken to the other since then.

Soop continued, "Pah's a mermaid, like me. Do you know what a mermaid is?

"Pah has arms and a tail and a head and a mouth with teeth and eyes and eyelids and a nose and lungs and gills." Soop gave up. "You'll know her from the others because she talks funny."

Soop had been speaking Mermish, but she wasn't sure the wand spoke it, so she repeated everything in the fairy-and-Clumsy tongue. At the end she said, "Make Pah apologize to me." She waved the wand.

Pah was sunning herself on Marooners' Rock. She sat up. Soop! Why had she waited so long to tell her best friend she was sorry? She dived into the lagoon.

Soop moved on to her second wish.

"A nautilus shell is a seashell," she told the wand. "It's the house, or maybe the skin, of a nautilus, which is a sea creature. You're in the sea right now, Sir Wand, a lagoon of the sea." At last she came to her command: "Make two nautilus shells, exactly the same size, and bring them to me. Make them just a tiny bit smaller than Queen Eewee's shell."

Mermaid rank is determined by the size of a mermaid's nautilus shell. Both Pah and Soop had medium-sized shells. Soop's shell was a little bigger than Pah's, so Soop was allowed to sit a little closer to the queen at dinner.

With the new shells, Soop and Pah would be equals, and they'd be much more important—duchesses, at least.

Soop waved the wand. Two enormous nautilus shells appeared at her feet. Before she had time to examine them, she heard Pah.

"*Aaaeeeiiiooouuuyyy!*" Trailing her orange scarf, Pah swam through the whalebone arch to Soop's room.

Soop swam out of her concealment forest.

"I'm sorry," Pah said. "It doesn't matter what the name of the song is. I can't tell yooo how sorry I am. I've been meaning tooo apologize. I don't know why I waited so long. Can yooo forgive me, Sooop?"

Soop hugged her. "I forgive you. Look!" She parted the seaweed in her concealment forest to reveal the shells.

Pah gasped. Soop thumped her tail in joy.

The nautilus shells were two-and-a-half feet long and plumply rounded. The center of one, the tightest part of its coil, was pearly with tints of pink and blue. The rest was creamy with emerald green stripes. The other was almond brown, shot through with splashes of pink and yellow.

"They're soooperb." Pah tried to be happy for her friend, but her jealousy leaked out. "Congratyooolations. I guess yooo'll want me to call yooo *Your Mership* from now on."

Soop was hurt. "Yes. You must. And I can write your name without a capital *p* whenever I like."

"Yooo may, although I don't know why yooo would write my name at all." She left Soop's room, calling over her shoulder, "You're tooo grand for me now."

Soop pulled the wand out of her concealment forest. "Make Pah come back," she whispered, and waved it. Then she dropped it back into the forest.

Pah swam backward, doing everything in reverse, until she faced Soop again. "How did I dooo that?"

"Silly, one shell is for you. Which do you want?"

"Really?"

Soop nodded.

Pah threw her arms around Soop's neck and thanked her. Then she swam down to the shells on the floor and examined them. The brown one was her favorite. It seemed merry and serious at the same time. It was a shell that knew how to have fun yet was still aware that there were sharks in the water. Pah was sure Soop preferred it, too, since it was the most beautiful shell in the world. Wanting to equal Soop's kindness, she said, "I'll take the striped one, unless yooo like it best."

Soop *did* like the striped one best. It was shell poetry, she thought, each color, each stripe, perfectly placed. But she wanted Pah to have her pick. "No," she said. "I adore the brown one."

"Done!" Pah said, swallowing her disappointment. "Sooon we'll be allowed tooo sing in Queen Eewee's inner chorus."

"Together," Soop said.

"Tooogether."

They smiled at each other.

"Where did yooo find the shells?"

Soop said, "Er . . . I have a magic wand."

A wand! Pah thought. She wondered when Soop had planned to tell her—and when Soop was going to let her use it.

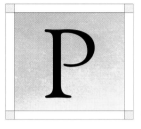

SIXTEEN

RILLA was on the ground near the nest, clearing the fairy circle of the stones that the flood had deposited there. That is, she sometimes cleared stones. More often, she turned cartwheels because the flood had ended and Sara Quirtle was complete.

After the water had drained away, Mother Dove's nest and the egg had been returned to their old branch, where Mother Dove was sure the egg was happiest.

Beck was on Mother Dove's back, picking out twigs and keeping an eye on the golden hawk. He was teaching himself to hunt mites, although he couldn't imagine a lowlier occupation.

Mother Dove saw Tink and Terence and Ree flying toward her. Terence had his arm around Tink, and they were flying one wing apiece, their glows connected.

He wasn't smiling, however. Tink wasn't either. Her face was as tragic as if all the pots in the world had vanished.

Mother Dove noticed that Ree's tiara was gone and that Ree seemed as shaken as Tink and Terence. Something terrible had happened.

Where was Rani?

Prilla called, "Hello, Tink!" She flew to them, surprised to see Terence, amazed to see them flying doubles. "Is Rani with Soop?"

Mother Dove moaned as the truth came to her. Rani was trapped inside a bat.

"I couldn't do anything," Ree said, weeping as copiously as Rani would have. "We saw her fly out of the water."

"Rani?" Prilla said, wondering why everyone was unhappy.

"She's a bat," Ree said.

Tink broke down. "We couldn't catch her. We don't . . ."

A bat! Prilla flew up and down from pure upsetness.

Beck knew what this meant. The bat would be in charge. Rani would have little influence over the logical bat temperament. Of all fairies, emotional Rani was the least suited for life within a bat.

"Tink was going to try to wake the wand up," Ree said, "so we could reverse our wishes. But now the wand is gone."

Prilla was glad they didn't know about Sara Quirtle. She didn't want that wish reversed.

"The hawks?" Beck asked Ree. "Did you do it?"

"She had wand madness," Terence said. "We all did."

"How could you? Look!" Beck pointed at the ground.

Ree saw the golden hawk. "They're alive!"

She sounded so relieved that Beck half forgave her.

"I might be able to blink to Rani," Prilla said. She'd blinked only to the mainland and to Fairy Haven, but her imaginary tunnel might take her anywhere.

"There are thousands of bats," Beck said. "How would you find Rani?"

Prilla blinked to a desk in the first row of a mainland classroom. Behind the teacher was a poster of a bat.

"This is the pear-tree bat," the teacher said. "It's our biggest bat."

That big? Prilla thought. The poster bat was almost half the size of the Clumsy teacher.

"Some scientists believe that fruit bats have a common ancestor with people." He replaced the poster of the pear-tree bat with a poster of a different bat. "This is the tiny masonry-hole bat."

It's just as big! Prilla thought. But it couldn't be.

"It's no bigger than your thumb."

A Clumsy's thumb, Prilla thought.

"Does anyone know the ancestor of the masonry-hole bat?" Prilla raised her hand. "Fairies?"

On Never Land, Beck asked Tink, "What kind of bat did Rani turn into?"

"A masonry-hole bat," Prilla said, half her mind still on the mainland.

Beck stared at her. "How do you know what a masonry-hole bat looks like? Did you see her?"

Prilla shook her head. "I just—sorry."

"Tink?"

Tink shrugged. "A bat."

"Ree? Terence?"

Terence shook his head. Ree said she didn't know.

"Brown? Gray? Tell me what to look for. Furry? Yellow-eyed? Round-eared? Tail—"

"A bat. Stop asking." Tink blamed herself for not noticing.

"Mother Dove?" Beck said. "Can I go after Rani?"

"Yes, dear."

Beck said, "I'll need a balloon carrier."

The golden hawk flew onto Beck's shoulder.

"I can pull the carrier," Prilla said.

Tink said, "Terence and I want to come, too."

Mother Dove said, "Tink, you may go. Terence . . . they need you to repair the canisters."

Tink pulled her bangs. "Mother—"

Mother Dove cooed at Tink, who finally nodded.

Beck said, "Tink, Prilla, let me talk to the bats. You won't know what should be said."

"If we find the right bat," Prilla said, "how do we turn her back into Rani?"

No one answered. Even Mother Dove didn't know.

SEVENTEEN

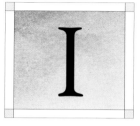

N THE ROTTING cherry tree, Rani tried to awaken Rani-bat, but Rani-bat was determined to remain asleep. The pinprick that was Rani shouted, Hey, bat! Let me out! Release me! I have to go back to the lagoon and warn Soop about the wand. I have to get out of you. Hey, bat! Wake up!

Rani-bat dreamed of hunting. In the dream, she crunched on a firefly. She swallowed it, but it didn't go down. Instead, it went up into her brain—a rude, unpleasant insect, whirring and shouting.

Rani felt the bat's awareness. She thought-shouted harder, louder. Wake up! Let me go! Bat! Bat! It's important! Set me free!

Rani-bat spoke and understood the fairy-and-Clumsy language, as all bats do. But she refused to listen to bad manners. She burrowed into a deeper sleep.

Rani felt the bat's awareness recede. How could she break through? She thought-screamed. She thought-shrieked. She thought-blasted.

Rani-bat slept on.

Prilla and Tink flew to Rani's room to fetch something for Rani to wear when—and if—she turned back into a fairy. Tink found the leafkerchief she'd given her, the one with a frying pan embroidered onto every corner. Prilla picked out Rani's six-pocket dress and selected five more leafkerchiefs. Tink nailed a tabletop across the hole Vidia had made in the ceiling, while Prilla fed Minnie, who had survived both the flood and the rain of plaster.

Beck waited outside with a balloon carrier that held a coconut shell and a sack of fairy dust. When Tink and Prilla arrived, they took the carrier cord and followed Beck toward the only two caves along the Wough River. The golden hawk tried to fly with them, but he couldn't keep up, so Beck stopped and let him perch on her head.

As they flew, Tink pictured Terence repairing a pumpkin canister. She was sure he was the best pumpkin-canister-repair fairy-dust talent in Never Land.

But Peter intruded on her thoughts. She imagined him reciting love songs to his clamshell.

"My guess," Beck said, "is that Rani is a nocturnal insectivorous Never bat."

"What's that?" Tink asked.

"It's an insect-eating night bat."

"Insect-eating?" Prilla cried.

"Yes." Beck half wished she herself had turned into a bat. It would be such an experience to be an animal.

"Why couldn't she be a pear-eating bat?" Prilla asked.

"Partly because there aren't as many fruit bats."

Prilla persisted. "Why else?"

"Just because." Beck had a hunch.

"Do we have to wait until dark to look for her?" Tink asked.

"We can't wait. At night she'll be out hunting. We have to hurry." The afternoon was half over.

"What if she isn't acting like a bat?" Tink asked.

Prilla said, "Then she'd have gone to Mother Dove."

"Or she might be wandering around somewhere, dazed," Beck said.

They hated to think about that.

While Pah seethed with hidden wand madness, Soop wanded up riches beyond the dreams of an ordinary mermaid, half for her and half for Pah: golden tail rings, rare combs, pirate plunder. Soop's concealment forest was so full of treasures that it glittered.

The two were lying back on Soop's sponge cushions, munching on kelp-jelly candies. Soop had never felt so much affection for her friend. She popped a jelly in Pah's mouth and one in her own. "Would you like to be queen? I could make you queen."

Pah didn't want to be queen. Too much work was involved. But she said, "I could make myself queen, if yooo'd let me wave the wand. Or I could make yooo queen."

Soop stroked the wand in her lap, wand madness rising in her, too. She dodged the issue. "I don't want to be queen."

"Then let me wave it for something else."

"I'll wave it for whatever you want. Tell me what you want."

"A wand."

Soop waved the wand. "Give Pah her own wand."

Nothing happened. A wand can't create another wand.

"Let me borrow yours. Please, Sooop. I just want tooo borrow it. I gave yooo my best scarf."

"I'll give you anything else. Tell me what you want."

Pah's anger bubbled up. She sprang off the cushions. "I want yooo tooo give yourself a tail rash."

Soop grew angry, too. "I'll give yooo—I mean *you*—a tail rash." Without noticing, she jiggled the wand. Luckily, her wording wasn't quite right. The wand didn't hear a command.

"I say tail rash," Pah sang nastily, "yooo say tail rash." She stopped singing. "Yooo can't even think of something different tooo give me."

"I'll give you . . . I'll give you . . ." Soop waved the wand, but she couldn't think of anything terrible enough.

"You're selfish and you're stooopid."

"You can't talk right." Soop was close to tears. "Yooo sound like a foool."

"Stooopid." Pah was close to tears, too.

"And you jerk your tail when you swim."

"I hate yooo." Pah regretted the words as soon as she said them. She'd never said anything so harsh before.

Soop felt as if Pah had slapped her. She put her hands over her ears, still holding the wand. "I wish not to be able to hear you ever again."

Pah swooped down on Soop's arm.

Soop hung onto the wand and finished the wish. "I wish no one else can hear you, either, no matter how loud you yell, ever again." With Pah clinging to her, Soop waved the wand.

EIGHTEEN

WHEN THEY reached the first cave at the edge of the Wough River, Beck tied the balloon carrier to a shrub outside. Prilla filled the coconut shell with river water, taking care not to get her wings wet. Tink lightened the shell with fairy dust, sprinkling the dust fondly, thinking of Terence. Then the three of them carried it into the cave.

The hawk stopped at the cave entrance. He'd been outside, under the sky, his whole life. He feared the cave walls closing in, and he blamed himself for being a coward.

Inside, Beck sensed a clutch of bats in a niche near the ceiling. "Up there," she whispered, pointing with her chin.

The fairies flew into the niche and set down the shell. Beck reveled in the bat smell. Tink and Prilla breathed through their mouths.

Beck spoke, adopting a flowery style foreign to fairy speech. "Pardon me, esteemed bats. So sorry to disturb your rest. We should have a letter of introduction. We should have made an appointment, but we happened to be nearby, and we wanted to pay our respects. Please accept this water as proof of our good wishes." She stepped back and gestured to Tink and Prilla that they should, too.

The matriarch bat unfurled her wings. She blinked in the light of fairy glow. "Welcome, Never fairies. Thank you for your gift." She flew to the water and sipped it.

Beck scrutinized the matriarch. She didn't think Rani could have become a matriarch this quickly. Still, Beck probed the matriarch's mind, where she sensed only bat thoughts.

The matriarch returned to her berth and to her sleep.

Although he was still frightened, the golden hawk flew to Beck. He thought he might detect something the fairies would miss.

Beck said, "Bats of every rank, please accept our gift. Please honor us by drinking."

The other bats awoke and lined up in size order.

Beck probed their minds and found nothing unbatlike. Still, she might not know. Rani might be jammed in so deep that even an animal talent couldn't tell.

The bats drank in turn.

Tink watched each one. She knew Rani so well—the brightness of her glow in the rain, her sniffle before reaching for a leafkerchief, her embarrassed smile while her eyes were brimming with tears. Tink was convinced all that couldn't be concealed by bat fur.

She didn't see the slightest trace of Raniness in any of the bats. Neither did Prilla. The hawk saw no hint of fairy.

Not a single bat lingered over the water. Not one showed any particular interest in the visitors.

Prilla kept trying to think of ways to turn a bat back into a fairy. She couldn't think of a thing, and she wondered whether it might be better to leave Rani where she was if they couldn't help her. But maybe she'd be happier with fairies, and how would they know?

The last bat drank and returned to bed. Beck signaled that they could leave, although she hated to go. They might be leaving Rani behind forever. "Farewell, esteemed bats."

Tears streaming, Pah rushed to Soop's desk. On Soop's sand slate she scratched, *I hate yooo!* She rubbed out *yooo!* and wrote *you!*

Soop was crying, too. She raised the wand and waved it. "I wish that you will no longer know how to write."

The sun was setting.

Beck, Tink, Prilla, and the golden hawk entered the second cave just as the bats began to wake up. The bats were too polite to refuse the fairies' water, but their minds were on the night ahead: where to meet their teammates and how to coordinate schedules—hunt moths at eight, hunt spiders at nine forty-five, take their first break at eleven, hunt fireflies at eleven twenty-five, present their progress reports at midnight.

The fairies and the hawk found not a whiff of Rani.

Pah threw herself facedown on Soop's bed, shoulders heaving. Soop lay next to her, weeping, too.

Half an hour passed as they cried themselves to sleep.

Night fell. Bat rush hour arrived.

Never Land's nocturnal bats streamed out of their caves and tree hollows. They wore no suits and carried no briefcases, but they were as businesslike as Clumsy efficiency experts.

For a while, Rani was almost happy. The rhythm of flight was familiar and comforting. The cool night air was delicious.

She tried to figure out where she was and where they were going. She couldn't identify any landmarks. Fairy Haven could be miles away or just over the next hill.

Oh, if only it were over the next hill! If only she could see the Home Tree! The Home Tree would light up her half-blind eyes.

Although she'd been inside a bat for half a day, she didn't understand bats at all. Rani-bat's eyes were open, and Rani could look through them, although shapes were blurry. But

Rani-bat didn't use her eyes much. She never moved them, never turned her head, just stared straight ahead.

Why didn't she bump into things? And why was she singing?

It was the most monotonous one-note song Rani had ever heard. *Beep-beep-beep-beep-beep.* No variation. *Beep-beep-beep-beep-beep.*

Wait! It broke off and started up. *B—p.* Rani-bat veered around a narrow tree trunk. The song changed again. *Bep-bep-bep-bep-bep.* Rani-bat flew through a clump of leaves.

That's funny, Rani thought. Although the note always felt the same in Rani-bat's throat, it didn't always sound the same.

Bee-ee-eep. Rani-bat flew up over a boulder.

Rani grasped what was happening. Rani-bat was finding her way by listening. She always sang the same *beeping* song. When it sounded different she knew something was nearby, and she knew exactly where and exactly what size.

Bat! Rani shouted. Bat, you have a talent! A talent!

Rani-bat barely heard.

Rani wished she could tell Tink or Beck. Tink, who loved to know how things worked, and Beck, who loved animals, would be captivated.

But she'd never tell them anything ever again.

B-b-b-b-b-eep!

Rani-bat put on a burst of speed. She thrust her head

forward. Her teeth snapped. She chewed once and swallowed the first insect of the night, a moth.

Ugh! Ugh! Ugh! Rani wanted to throw up. If she'd had her own stomach she would have. *Ick!* She was beside herself. How could you? she screamed. I'm in here, too. The pinprick that she was writhed and shuddered.

Rani-bat nabbed another moth.

BECK HOVERED above the balloon carrier, still parked on the bank of the Wough River. "We might as well sleep. There's nowhere to look until morning." She landed and stretched out under the broad leaf of a Never cabbage. Prilla joined her. Tink curled up under a large toadstool.

Prilla was asleep as soon as her eyes closed. Sara Quirtle paddled a canoe through the ocean. Prilla sat on the prow. Mermaid hands appeared on the sides of the canoe and began to pull it under. Sara Quirtle hit the hands with her paddle. Prilla pried a finger away. More hands appeared. The boat capsized. Prilla's wings took on water. She was drowning!

She sat up. She'd never been in a nightmare before. But if Sara Quirtle was having such a lively nightmare, she was still complete. Prilla fell asleep again, entering calmer Clumsy dreams.

When she was sure the others were sleeping, Tink flew out from under the toadstool. After half an hour she reached the forest above Peter's underground home. She descended through

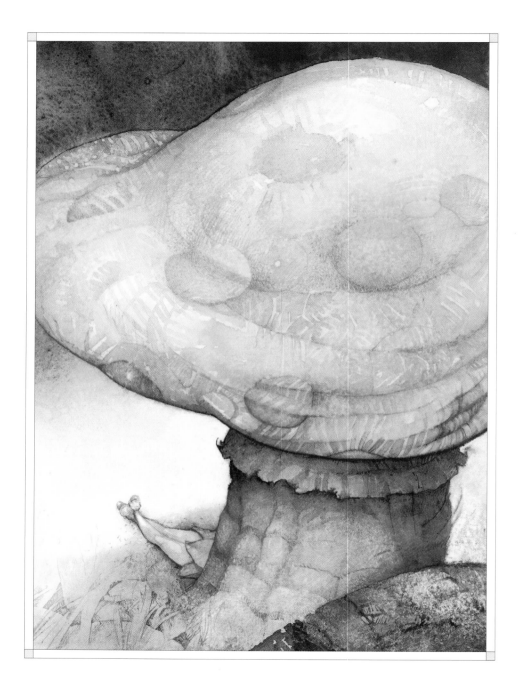

Peter's tree and hovered, unseen, her glow lost in the fireplace's flickering light.

The Lost Boys sprawled on the big bed, watching Peter, who flew above them.

Tink's wings fluttered in double time. She remembered a hundred scenes just like this one.

"There are many clamshells," Peter said, holding out a clamshell, "but I chose this one."

"It is a superior clamshell," the Lost Boy Slightly said. "I saw that immediately."

Tink pulled her bangs. Slightly had always irritated her.

"It whispers secrets in my ear." Peter held it to his ear.

The Lost Boy Tootles said, "Might I listen?"

Peter held it to Tootles's ear.

"I don't hear anything, Peter."

"It speaks only to me. It says the most extraordinary things."

Tink flew up Peter's tree and back toward Prilla and Beck. Peter would be more likely to hear the clamshell reciting love songs to him than the other way around. She should have known.

Terence was different. Better.

Inside Rani-bat, Rani gave up screaming and suffered in silence. She couldn't decide if the worst aspect of the bug banquet was the insects that tasted bad or the insects that tasted good. Spiders were disgusting. Their legs were sharp and hurt going down. She kept expecting to choke to death. Their soft middles were mushy and tasted like putrid cheese. Rani-bat seemed to like the spiders, though. She ate a whole dozen.

Wasps, on the other hand, which you'd expect to be dry and bitter, were sweet and juicy. Rani could have eaten a hundred. Of course, it didn't matter what she wanted. Either Rani-bat didn't like them, or they were hard to catch. She ate only two.

Moths reminded Rani of acorn chips. Fireflies were sour. Ladybugs tickled the roof of Rani-bat's mouth. Midges were bursts of pepper. Yummy or yucky, however, eating bugs was more embarrassing than anything Rani could imagine.

She tried to distract herself with pleasant thoughts, but they all turned unpleasant. She thought of her talent—she'd never use it again. She thought of Soop—she had failed to tell her about the permanence of a wish. She thought of Tink and Prilla—they must miss her dreadfully, and she missed them dreadfully. She thought of Mother Dove, and that was the worst of all. Never again to hear Mother Dove's coos or be folded into her soft feathers. Why, she might as well dissolve into the bat.

Rani thought that not one Never fairy wand wish had been either sensible or harmless. The only good the quest might have done was to end the flood. She wished she knew it had ended.

That was a harmless wish—just to know—wasn't it?

She couldn't tell. She wasn't sure if wishes were bad or wands were bad, or only sleeping wands, or only irreversible wishes. If she'd had her own head, she'd have had a headache.

Worn out, miserable, drier than wing powder, Rani fell asleep.

In Fairy Haven, Mother Dove yearned to visit every matriarch bat, one after the other, and beg, mother-to-mother, for help. They'd understand. They'd locate the bat that used to be Rani. When Mother Dove had her, she'd find a way, somehow, to change her back.

She'd also fly to Marooners' Rock and get a message to

Soop. She'd persuade her to return the wand. Then she'd fly it to the mainland and make Tutupia reverse each wish.

Instead, she had to stay on the egg, eternally on the egg, while her fairies were in danger.

Shortly before dawn, the golden hawk pecked Beck's arm. Beck sat up. She woke Tink and Prilla.

"Rani's bat may have found a home closer to the shore," she said. "We'll fly toward the lagoon."

Along with the rest of her colony, Rani-bat began the flight back to the cherry tree. She'd had a good night. She'd eaten eighty insects in seven categories and had been complimented by her team leader.

Rani woke up and was shocked again when she realized where she was. She noticed how full her bat stomach felt. *Ugh!*

Soop was facing away from Pah when she awoke. The light in the lagoon never changed much, so she listened to see if it was morning. Yes, mermaid servants were moving about in the kitchen. She sat up and saw Pah.

Memories flooded in. Where was the wand? Ah. She saw saw it, half-hidden by her scarf. She picked it up and settled back into her pillows.

Pah is so pretty, Soop thought. No one else had such fine hair or as long a tail. She loved the trusting way Pah's hand curled in her sleep. Soop decided she'd reverse the spells as soon as Pah opened her eyes. They'd make up, and then they could play a game of Sirens Sink Ships, if Pah wanted to.

The three fairies and the hawk soared over a stretch of scrubland halfway to the lagoon. As they flew, they observed the destinations of colony after colony of homeward-bound bats. Prilla marveled at how careful the bats were. They stayed within one another's wingspans, but they never collided and never missed a wing stroke.

Shortly before her colony reached home, Rani-bat and the fairies passed each other, flying not four feet apart.

Even with her terrible bat vision, Rani saw the balloon carrier. Was it her carrier? The one she had gone to the mainland in?

A fairy had to be pulling it, but what she saw looked like two splotches. Another splotch flew nearby. Who were they? Was it a coincidence? Or were the fairies looking for her?

She tried to cry out. Hey! It's me, Rani! Look! I'm not a bat! She tried so hard she made Rani-bat's eyes protrude the tiniest bit.

Beck made note of the swarm entering the cherry tree. It

was a sizable bunch, worth investigating later. She flew on. Prilla and Tink followed.

A bigger swarm flew into the hollow under a fallen hemlock. Beck made another note. The three of them could spend years bringing water to bats. Years, and they might never find Rani.

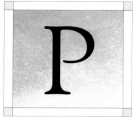AH WOKE UP and smiled at Soop. She mouthed *good morning* and was surprised for a moment when no sound emerged.

Soop said, "Make Pah able to speak again so that everyone can hear her, including me. Make her know how to write." She waved the wand. "Good morning, Pah."

Good morning.

Soop frowned. Pah looked frightened.

"Reverse my commands about Pah speaking and writing." Soop waved the wand.

Can yooo hear me?

The fairies and the hawk spent the morning in three bat residences and found not the slightest suggestion of Rani. At noon they entered the cherry tree where Rani-bat was sleeping and where Rani was awake and bored.

Rani heard the coconut shell *thunk* down on the rotting floor of the residence. She wondered what was happening, but Rani-bat's eyes were closed, and they wouldn't help much anyway. Then she heard Beck.

"Pardon me, esteemed bats. So sorry . . ."

Rani started screaming. Wake up! There are fairies here! Wake up! Beck's here! Wake up!

It was that firefly again! Rani-bat pushed the annoying voice away.

". . . to disturb your rest. We know we should have a letter of introduction. Furthermore, we should have petitioned . . ."

Rani screamed *Wake up!* three more times and then stopped to hear what Beck was saying.

". . . we should have made an appointment, but we happened to be nearby, and we wanted to pay our respects."

Rani-bat woke up. Someone had come in and was speaking reasonably. The someone's voice sounded like the firefly's voice. Rani-bat raised her head.

The golden hawk, who could spot movement better than anyone, saw Rani-bat's head bob.

"Please accept this water as proof of our good wishes." Beck stepped away from the coconut shell.

The matriarch bat spread her wings. "Welcome, Never fairies. Thank you for bringing us water." She flew to the shell and drank. Then she returned to her sleep station.

Beck said, "Bats of every rank, please accept our gift. Please honor us by drinking."

The other bats awoke. In their calm, unruffled way, they lined up in size order. Rani-bat was two-thirds down the line.

Rani spoke softly to the bat surrounding her, imitating Beck. Pardon me, esteemed bat. She felt she was betraying the fairy way, but she went on. We haven't been introduced, but I beg the favor of your attention.

The firefly had learned manners! Rani-bat listened.

Rani felt the bat's attention. I am Rani, honored bat, a water-talent fairy. Yesterday I turned into you when a mermaid—

Preposterous! The firefly was only pretending to have manners. Rani-bat turned her mind away.

Rani felt the change, but she continued to speak in the new polite fashion. She hoped something was getting through.

A bit was. Politeness appeals powerfully to bats.

Soop worded her commands to the wand in dozens of ways to try and reverse what she'd done to Pah. Pah twisted her scarf in her hands and tried to speak and write after every attempt.

It occurred to Soop that Pah might be the only one able to reverse the commands. Soop still didn't want to give up the wand, but she couldn't bear Pah's distress, or her own, any longer.

She held out the wand. "You try it. Maybe the one who's been wished on can reverse the wishes."

How can I command the wand when I can't speak?

Soop couldn't read lips, but she guessed what Pah had asked. "Maybe you only have to think the command, or maybe it will work if you mouth the words."

Pah decided to try a different wish first, to see if her commands would be obeyed: *send breakfast for Sooop and me.*

A breakfast tray floated through Soop's door. Pah hardly paid attention to what was on it: scrambled roe, toasted flatfish bread, clam juice, and two mugs of hot squid ink—Pah's black, seal milk in Soop's. The tray settled on Soop's walk-the-plank dining table.

Make everyone able tooo hear me, and make me able tooo write. Pah waved the wand. *Can yooo hear me?*

"I can't hear you."

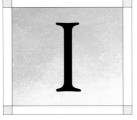I T WAS RANI-BAT'S turn to drink from the coconut shell. The bat felt Rani's keen pleasure in the water and took three more sips than any other bat had. Both Tink and the golden hawk noticed. Tink nudged Prilla, who nudged Beck.

Rani-bat started back to bed.

Rani spoke softly, squelching her desire to shout. Esteemed bat, please don't return to your sleeping place so quickly. I love water. Before I made your esteemed acquaintance, I had an ability with water. . . . She thought of how to say what she wanted: I cannot write a petition. I don't know how to make a formal entreaty, but I beg you most humbly to return for a few more sips. Wondering if she was overdoing the politeness, Rani repeated *most humbly*. . . .

Rani-bat slowed.

That was enough for the golden hawk. Mustering his courage, he flew to Rani-bat and perched on her head.

Rani-bat jerked her head back and snapped.

The hawk whirred to the residence entrance and hovered

there with a gash in his leg that bled onto the wood floor.

Tink drew her knife, in case the bat came after the hawk. Then she sheathed it. The bat might be Rani.

Beck flew to him, and he let her look at his wound and pat fairy dust on it. Then she flew to Rani-bat, who had returned to the coconut shell.

"Esteemed bat, my friends and I . . ."

Friends? Rani thought. Tink? Prilla? Were they here, too? Oh! Oh!

". . . are searching for a particular bat. Pardon the unexpectedness of my request, but might we have a conversation?"

Rani-bat turned her head toward the matriarch, wondering if she'd mind.

The matriarch was asleep.

"Esteemed fairy, I suppose it will be all right," Rani-bat said.

Beck led Rani-bat and Tink and Prilla to a corner of the residence. As Rani-bat followed Beck, Rani said, Esteemed bat, these are my friends. I hope you'll like them, too.

Like and dislike matter little to Never bats.

"Esteemed bat . . ." Beck took a deep breath and hoped her strategy would work. "I am Beck of the animal-talent Never fairies. This is Tinker Bell of the pots-and-pans talent, and this is Prilla of the clapping and mainland-blinking talent. May I have the honor of knowing your name?"

"I am pleased to make your acquaintance. My name is—" Rani-bat stopped, as Beck hoped she would. Rani-bat realized for the first time she didn't know her own name.

Rani said, Esteemed bat, you are welcome to use my name. My name is Rani.

"Esteemed Beck, my name may be Rani."

Tink wanted to turn one of Prilla's cartwheels. Prilla, afraid of startling the bat, confined herself to jumping two inches into the air.

"I look forward to flying with you, esteemed Rani," Beck said.

"I look forward to flying with you, esteemed Rani," Prilla echoed, forgetting that Beck had told her not to speak.

"Fly with you," Tink said, forgetting, too.

Rani wanted to weep happy tears. Fly with you, esteemed Tink and Prilla and Beck. Fly with you!

Beck said, "I know a Never fairy whose name is Rani. She is of the water-talent fairies." Beck probed Rani-bat's mind and found significant unease. If the bat became more distressed, she might stop talking. Beck tried to make her feel more comfortable. "I hope your hunt was successful last night."

Tink tugged her bangs. What was Beck waiting for?

"My hunt was successful."

Beck said, "I am glad to hear it."

Tink burst out, "We're here because our friend Rani is missing. Rani is very emotional—"

Wanting to throttle Tink, Beck said, "Hush, esteemed Tink."

But Tink didn't hear. "—and sometimes she carries things too far, but she's the kindest fairy in Fairy Haven, and she'll do anything for a friend, and she's the best water-talent fairy there is." She stopped. It was the longest speech she'd ever made.

Oh, Tink! Rani wished she could hug her.

Rani-bat disliked outbursts.

Prilla made it worse by saying, "Rani didn't mean to become a bat."

"Honorable fairies, I will return to bed now," Rani-bat said. Fairies turning into bats had nothing to do with her. She began to fly.

Tink wanted to slap herself. She'd ruined everything.

Rani begged, Please, esteemed bat, listen to my friends. Please talk to them. Um, esteemed bat, if you do, I'll teach you to use water to catch insects.

That had an effect. Rani-bat flapped her wings uncertainly. Two wasps had gotten away last night, and she'd been furious.

Beck flew after Rani-bat. She had decided to use shock. "Esteemed bat, what is your earliest memory?"

Rani-bat landed in the center of the residence floor. Tink and Prilla flew close enough to hear, but far enough away to be inconspicuous.

"A mermaid was singing. I don't care for music. I was in the sea."

"When was that, esteemed bat?" Beck said.

"A long time ago. When I was born."

Esteemed bat, Rani said, it was yesterday.

Yes, Rani-bat thought. It was yesterday. I wasn't born yesterday, was I?

Rani said, Esteemed bat, don't you remember being laughed up? Don't you remember blowing over the sea to Never Land? Don't you remember wanting to touch the water on the way? You had your talent already, even though you were still just a laugh. Don't you remember?

Rani-bat wasn't certain. The events did sound familiar. She

was so startled she spoke out loud. "I think I may be a fairy. There is certainly a fairy inside me." Then, for the first time, she spoke to Rani in her mind. But I'm also a bat.

I know, Rani said. Esteemed bat, it's a mess.

TWENTY-TWO

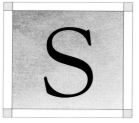

OOP SAID, "Pah, wish something terrible on me. I deserve it. Take away my new nautilus shell. Turn me into a sea urchin or a tuna's tooth, or whatever you like." Soop closed her eyes and waited, terrified and brave.

Pah mouthed, *I could turn yooo intooo the biggest nautilus shell ever, or the smallest. I could turn yooo intooo a speck of sand.* But those wouldn't suit what Soop had done to her. She drank her squid ink, ate a slice of toast, and thought until she arrived at the perfect revenge.

Make Sooop unable tooo hear anything anyone says tooo her. Make her unable tooo read. She raised the wand.

Rani-bat conceded that since she was really a fairy she should have a fairy's body. It was logical, but . . .

"Esteemed Rani-bat," Beck said, "will you allow Rani-fairy to become herself again?"

Yes! Esteemed bat, I beg of you, please say *yes*.

Rani-bat didn't answer Beck or Rani. She didn't want to lose herself.

"Esteemed Rani-bat," Beck said, "will you favor me with a reply?"

Tink had once fixed a teapot that had turned itself into a coffeepot. Its owner hadn't wanted a coffeepot, but the coffeepot wouldn't change back until Tink had made a metal coffee bean to adorn the teapot lid.

"Beck? Can I talk to you?" Tink didn't want to risk offending the bat again.

Beck came over.

Tink whispered, "Maybe Rani could let the bat live inside her. They could change places."

"Excellent!" Beck made the suggestion to Rani-bat.

Rani-bat pondered for a long minute. It was fair, but she'd have to give up her body, her song, her authority. The fairy would be in charge, and Rani-bat had noticed that the fairy was less than logical.

Still, it was right for Rani to have her fairy form back. Finally, she asked Rani, Will you let me stay inside you?

If Rani had had her own throat, she would have gulped. She wanted to be rid of the bug-eating politeness maniac. She didn't want to carry Rani-bat around forever.

But she said yes. Of course she said yes, and she said it

gratefully and graciously. Rani-bat was making an enormous sacrifice. Rani planned to cry for her as soon as she could. Esteemed bat, she said, I will be honored to have you within me.

Rani-bat said, "Esteemed Beck, I won't stop Rani-fairy from becoming herself again." She paused, then said, "How is it done?" She wondered, with a flutter in her belly, if it was painful.

Yes, how is it done? Rani thought. She didn't care how much it hurt.

Beck was silent.

"Esteemed fairy, you don't know?"

You don't know? Rani screamed.

Rani-bat was relieved. "I shall return to my rest, esteemed fairies."

"Wait! Er . . . Please wait!" Beck said. "Esteemed Rani-bat, please allow me a moment to think."

Prilla approached Beck. "Maybe clapping would help."

Beck nodded. It might. "We're going to try something, esteemed Rani-bat."

Prilla was in Sara Quirtle's nursery-school playroom. "Clap if you believe in Rani the fairy." Sara Quirtle led the clapping, and the other Clumsy children followed.

Prilla flew over a line of Clumsy children waiting to ride on a roller coaster. "Clap if you believe in Rani the fairy."

Rani felt a surge of energy. She was still a pinprick, but she had some power. She buzzed inside Rani-bat's brain.

"Did it work?" Prilla asked.

"Do you feel any change, esteemed Rani-bat?" Beck said.

"Esteemed fairies, I feel a churning . . ." Rani-bat touched her wing to her temple. ". . . here. It's tunneling down. Perhaps it will fly through my mouth."

"Come, Rani!" Tink shouted. "Come out!"

Rani felt herself floundering near the top of Rani-bat's throat. Then she fell, down Rani-bat's windpipe into her chest. She tried to rise again but couldn't.

"I'll do more." Prilla blinked away.

Beck thought about tadpoles. She had helped several turn into frogs. Perhaps that technique would succeed now.

Beck said, "May I speak to Rani-fairy, esteemed Rani-bat?"

"Honorable Beck, she hears you."

Beck said the words that had set the tadpoles going. "Push! Push!"

Rani tried to push, but she didn't have enough substance to push with. She remained a pinprick.

"Honorable Beck, Rani-fairy is too small to push."

Prilla jumped out of a Clumsy magician's hat. She shouted to the audience of Clumsy children, "Clap if you believe in Rani the fairy."

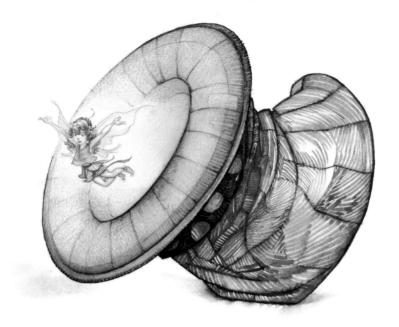

Rani gained more power, but not enough.

Tink flew to Beck. "Maybe fairy dust will help."

After obtaining Rani-bat's permission, Beck sprinkled her with fairy dust. The dust did help.

"Esteemed fairies, she's growing!"

Rani pushed. She swelled to the size of an acorn and then stopped. With enormous effort, and with the help of the dust and the clapping, she found her voice and propelled it through Rani-bat's throat. "Help! I'm stuck."

"Rani!" Tink cried, elated to hear her friend's voice. "Oh, Rani!"

"Esteemed fairies," Rani-bat said, "I apologize for complaining, but she's a lump now, and she's hurting me."

Beck sprinkled on more fairy dust. Rani grew again and then became stuck again, and a whole cup more fairy dust did no good. Prilla persuaded more Clumsy children to clap, but their clapping had done as much as it could.

The hawk landed on Beck's head. "If the bat won't bite me, I will fly to her. My feathers may help."

Beck said, "Esteemed Rani-bat. This is the golden hawk. He is not an insect. He regrets he has no letter of introduction. He wishes he had an appointment. He may be able to help Rani-fairy emerge. May he approach and do what he can?"

Rani-bat consented.

The hawk flew to Rani-bat. He spread his wings. The golden underside of his feathers gleamed in the dimness of the residence. He brushed the gold against the fur on Rani-bat's back.

Rani felt her power grow. She pushed. She swelled until she filled Rani-bat's chest and stomach. Rani-bat's wings tingled.

The hawk ran the gold of his feathers across Rani-bat's face and belly. He flew back to the residence entryway.

Rani pushed.

TWENTY-THREE

AH had held the wand, her hand raised, unmoving, for the last ten minutes while she considered her friend, next to her on the bed, eyes squeezed shut, face blank with fear.

Finally, Pah dropped the wand. She hugged Soop. *I can't dooo anything bad tooo yooo.*

Rani pushed.

Rani-bat's wings curled into themselves and re-formed as arms and fingers. Her fur fell to the floor in clumps. Rani's wand-inspired wings sprouted from her shoulders. Rani-bat's scalp itched ferociously as hair grew there. Finally, Rani-bat's eyes changed, and they filled with tears, and Rani was back.

She fell into Tink's arms and wept and laughed. Tink patted her awkwardly, feeling as happy to see Rani as Rani was to be seen.

Prilla returned from blinking. "Rani's here!" She turned a cartwheel, then flew out to the balloon carrier for Rani's dress.

"The flood! Did it go down? Is Fairy Haven dry?"

"Yes," Tink said. "It's dry." She guided Rani's wings through the dress's wing slits.

"I'm so glad you found me. I thought no one would come."

Inside her, Rani-bat said, Esteemed fairy, I suggest you say *thank you.*

Rani's glow turned pink. "Rani-bat wants me to thank you, and you know I do."

Tink and Beck looked uncomfortable.

Prilla said, "You're very welcome."

Rani turned to the golden hawk, heeding Rani-bat's urging. "Thank you."

He inclined his head majestically.

Tink said, "Did you tell Soop that wishes are—"

"—permanent?" Rani shook her head, scattering tears. "No. I was enjoying myself too much. Then, when she started to sing, I couldn't. I'll go now, but it's probably too late."

"Rani . . ." Tink said. "You have to get the wand—"

"—back. Back? I do?" She felt the stirrings of wand greed. "Then I will."

A magic wand, esteemed fairy?

Tink sensed Rani's eagerness. "You can't use—"

"—it." Rani recognized her symptoms. "I'll want to use it. I don't want to want to, but I'll want to."

"Bring it to Mother Dove," Beck said. "Keep thinking, I have to bring it to Mother Dove."

Rani echoed, "Bring it to Mother Dove."

"At the nest, I'll try to wake it up," Tink said.

"I may be able to help," Beck said. "I think a wand may be like a dormouse."

"Then we'll reverse the wishes," Tink said.

"Not my Sara Quirtle wish!" Prilla said.

The others looked at Prilla.

She blushed. "I waved the wand. When you were pulling the balloon carrier, before I helped you. Remember?" She told them her wish.

Rani hugged her. "You *do* have a talent for being sweet."

Tink would have hugged her, too, if she'd been prone to hugging. Prilla had made the only wish that didn't need fixing. "I won't reverse your wish. After I reverse the others, we have to return the wand to the Great—"

"—Wandies." Rani nodded.

"But," Beck said, "will Soop give you the wand?"

"Maybe mermaids don't get wand madness," Prilla said.

Tink tugged her bangs. "Soop sent us a flood to get a wand. What does that sound like?"

Pah mouthed very slowly, *Drink your squid ink, Sooop*. She

pantomimed drinking, with her thumb straight up, which is the way mermaids drink squid ink.

Soop thought Pah wanted more hot ink, so she wanded up some more. A silver urn wrapped in a towel appeared on the breakfast tray.

Pah shook her head. She pointed at Soop. *Yooo drink.*

"I drink?"

Pah nodded.

"I understood you?"

Pah smiled.

Soop smiled back. "We can talk without talking, right?"

Pah nodded. *Now drink.*

"What?"

At the edge of the residence, Rani-bat said, Esteemed fairy, before we leave, you must thank the matriarch, who kindly took us in when we had no home.

Tell me what to say.

Please tell me what to say.

Rani sighed. Please tell me what to say.

Blushing, Rani spoke as Rani-bat dictated. "Esteemed matriarch, thank you for your hospitality. I shall revere your memory forever."

She stepped outside, and, for the first time, Rani-bat saw the world with Rani's excellent eyesight.

Oh! Oh! Rani-bat cried. What is that, esteemed fairy?

Rani smiled. Those are cherry blossoms, esteemed bat.

What's that, esteemed fairy?

Rani's happy tears flowed again. That's the blue sky, esteemed bat.

What's that, esteemed—

—fairy? That's the sun, esteemed bat.

What's that, esteemed—

—fairy? That's a green leaf, esteemed bat.

Esteemed fairy, it's rude to interrupt. What's that, esteemed—

—fairy? Oops! That's a fly, esteemed bat.

Rani wasn't ready for Rani-bat's response. Rani's head jerked forward. She snapped at the fly and missed, to her great relief.

Don't do that! Esteemed bat, fairies don't eat bugs.

"Rani?" Prilla said.

"I'm fine."

What do they eat, if I might ask, esteemed . . .

Rani conquered the impulse to interrupt.

. . . fairy?

We eat honey, esteemed bat, and other food.

Esteemed fairy, honey is not a bee.

Beck said she was leaving to tell Mother Dove that Rani had been restored. She flew off, with the golden hawk on her head.

Prilla, Tink, and Rani flew toward the lagoon. On the way, Rani shared her memories concerning the wand with Rani-bat.

Esteemed fairy, when you get the wand, would you set me free?

Rani wondered if bats were susceptible to wand madness, too. I must have the wand, esteemed bat, before I decide what to do with it.

They arrived at the lagoon.

Tink said, "We'll meet you at the nest." She didn't trust herself to be there when Rani emerged with the wand. She was already thinking of wishes. Terence could replace Ree. He'd be a perfect king.

"Don't go, Rani!" Prilla wrung her hands. "Soop could sing again. She could wave—"

"She has to go," Tink said.

"I have to." She dived.

TWENTY-FOUR

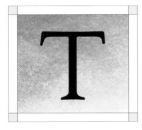TAILS SWISHING, Soop and Pah faced each other, floating above Soop's walk-the-plank table.

Soop yelled, "Move your lips slower!"

I'm moooving them so slowly they're getting cramps.

Of course, this was not a simple sentence to decipher.

"What?"

Mermaids swam along the corridor outside Soop's room. No one paid attention to Soop's shouts or Pah's pantomimes. Soop and Pah were always playing or quarreling. No one noticed the wand, either, lying next to the squid-ink mugs on the table.

I . . . Pah pointed to herself. . . . *think* . . . Pah tapped her head.

"You . . ." Soop pointed at Pah. ". . . think," Soop said. "Right?"

Rani swam in just beneath Soop's ceiling and just above Soop and Pah, whose bodies blocked the wand from sight. Neither mermaid saw Rani.

Pah nodded. . . . *You're* . . . She pointed at Soop. . . . *not* . . . She mouthed the word *trying* very slowly.

"I am so trying!"

Esteemed fairy, I don't see a wand.

Esteemed bat, that one's my friend. Rani pointed. I should greet her, esteemed bat. It's only polite.

If you greet the mermaid, esteemed fairy, she probably won't give you the wand.

Pah blew Soop a kiss. *Good*. They had worked out that blowing a kiss meant *good*.

"Say something else," Soop said.

I still want to share the wand.

"What?" Soop said.

Rani breaststroked to Soop's concealment forest and saw the heap of tail rings, combs, and doubloons.

Esteemed fairy, we'll spend hours searching in there. Please look elsewhere first.

Pah pointed at herself. *I* . . .

"I?"

Pah nodded and skipped the word *still* as too hard. . . . *want* . . . She clasped her hands to her chest.

"What?"

Pah clasped her hands to her chest again and mouthed *want* very slowly.

"Want?"

Pah blew a kiss.

"I got 'want'!" Soop was delighted. She clasped her hands to her chest. "This means 'want'! What do you want?"

Rani tried to lift Soop's pillow, but it was too heavy. She swam down to the reed rug. No wand. She snaked upward.

"You want us to do something?" Soop said.

Share. Pah gestured back and forth between them.

"What?"

Rani swam over Soop's wicker bureau.

There it is! Esteemed fairy, I see it with my—your— our—eyes. Rani-bat had never found anything by sight before.

Rani swam to the wand. She held it tight against her body, stroked her wings, and kicked her feet as hard as she could. She swam out through Soop's archway.

Frustrated, Pah dived down to the table for the wand. She pushed the plates and mugs aside. *It's gone! The wand is gone!*

"What?"

Fairies collected around the nest to wait for Rani's return. They simmered with wand madness. Even Beck was infected. She sat on a branch several yards from the nest. She wouldn't come closer lest Mother Dove sense her nonstop wishing for the power to switch to any animal—bear, beaver, butterfly—and back to fairy, whenever she liked.

On a branch above Mother Dove, Ree straightened her second-best tiara. She was dreaming again of declaring herself empress and wielding the wand as her scepter.

Prilla was there, too, just back from another blink to Sara Quirtle. Prilla alone was untouched by wand madness. Perhaps she was too new to have collected many wishes, or she was too pleased with the wish she had made to want more.

"Prilla . . ." Mother Dove said.

Prilla flew to the nest.

"Fetch Vidia from her room. Tell her not to argue."

Prilla flew off, certain that Vidia would argue.

"Mother Dove?" Tink called from her perch below the nest, next to Terence. "We don't need Vidia."

"Maybe not," Mother Dove said. She wasn't sure which fairy would be needed. She wasn't sure if any of them would succeed with the wand.

Never fear, she thought to the egg. There is nothing to fear.

Terence took Tink's hand.

"If you were a cake pan," Tink told him tenderly, "your cakes would be delicious, even if a doorknob-talent fairy made them."

"If you were fairy dust," Terence said, "you would come from Mother Dove's neck."

Tink's glow deepened at the compliment. Then she sighed. "I may not be able to wake the wand. The Great Wandies said we couldn't."

"You'll do it."

"I may not be able to reverse the wishes."

"You'll be able to."

"I may not reverse your wish."

"Reverse it," Terence said bravely. "We're both broken pots

now. You're the Tink who has to care about me, and I'm the Terence who made you have to care."

"I'll miss you." Tink tugged her bangs. "But I won't know it."

Terence reached into the pocket of his frock coat. "Take this." He gave her a small velvet pouch. "It's leg dust. Use it on your most contrary pots."

Tink dimpled. "The desperate cases."

"That's right."

"After I use the dust, I'll keep the pouch." She hooked it onto her belt, next to her dagger. "I'll save it forever."

Terence doubted she would, but he said, "That will be lovely."

They sat together quietly. Tink stopped worrying about the ordeal ahead. Terence's company was as soothing as copper polish.

Rani swam out of the mermaid's castle and upward through the lagoon.

Esteemed fairy, please set me free.

Rani didn't answer. She rose out of the water and began to fly toward Fairy Haven.

Please let me be a bat again.

Rani would have loved to be rid of Rani-bat, but she didn't dare. She heard every one of Rani-bat's thoughts, which were about snatching the wand and waving it and becoming a bat matriarch and drawing thousands of spiders to her and eating them. Thanking Rani was part of Rani-bat's plan, but giving up the wand wasn't.

TWENTY-FIVE

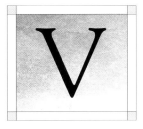IDIA DIDN'T answer Prilla's knocks, so Prilla eased the door open.

"Step right in, darling. Don't wait for an invitation."

Prilla sneezed. The room could have belonged to a wrecking-talent fairy. Wing-chair stuffing drifted in the air. Strips of cloth from Vidia's wing-patterned bed canopy dangled over the bed. Black paint blotches splashed across the cloud mural on Vidia's west wall.

"Vidia?" Prilla flew to the bed.

Vidia rolled over, facedown.

"Mother Dove wants you to come to the nest."

Silence.

"Mother Dove said not to argue."

Vidia turned her head to the side to speak. "Am I arguing, love?"

"No, but you haven't come."

Silence.

Vidia would have come instantly if Prilla had told her that

Tink was going to try to reverse everyone's wishes. But Prilla didn't know about Vidia's wish.

"Mother Dove must have a good reason for wanting you."

"Honeybunch, the only reason . . ." Vidia turned on her side. Maybe Mother Dove thought she could get her old flight back. She sprang up, and was gone.

Prilla followed, wondering what she'd said to make Vidia change her mind.

Fighting wand madness, Rani passed over beach, brush, and the woods that bordered Fairy Haven. She passed over the Home Tree, the barnyard, the mill, and the orchard and reached the air high above Mother Dove's hawthorn. There, her own madness and Rani-bat's joined forces. She didn't descend.

Mother Dove felt her up there. She raised her beak and began to coo resounding coos that filled her tree, expanded to the fairy circle, and rose to the clouds above. Rani heard them. Her madness didn't drain away, but it shrank and became manageable. The madness of the assembled fairies shrank, too.

Esteemed fairy, a bird is your matriarch?

She's Mother Dove, esteemed bat.

"Give the wand to Tink," Mother Dove cooed.

Tink and Terence had flown to the ground under the hawthorn.

"You can fix anything," Terence said and stepped back.

Rani handed the wand to Tink.

Fairies circled Tink or hovered above her. Tink sprinkled fairy dust on the wand, remembering Tutupia's hope that they had picked one with a big heart. If they hadn't, Tink wanted to expand the heart before she woke the wand. She held the wand in one hand and ran her other hand along its length. As before, the wand was aware of her power.

The cottony layers of sleep blocked Tink's view of the heart. Her fingers barely moving, she began to lift away the layers, intending to remove just a few. As she did, the wand wriggled and shed layers, too. She glimpsed its pinched heart and malicious mind just as the wand threw off its last wisp of sleep.

It jerked Tink along the ground. She hung on, concentrating, probing the heart for a soft spot. *Oof!* They slammed into Terence, who grasped the wand to steady it, to help Tink.

He shouldn't have put a finger on it. It could do nothing unless someone held it, and it didn't want to be held by Tink. It yanked itself away from her but clung to him. Tink sprawled on the ground. He tried to get to her, but the wand wouldn't let him.

Mother Dove sang in tinkling, plinking notes, the way one wand might sing to another. "These are my fairies, wand. Please be kind."

If its heart hadn't been weak, the wand would have been happy to be kind. It heard Mother Dove's words but didn't heed them. It was bent on mischief! It lifted Terence onto Mother Dove's back.

The moment Terence touched Mother Dove, the wand sniffed out her wish: that her chick would hatch. Mother Dove didn't wish her wish. She didn't even think of it. Her only thoughts were for her fairies. But the wish was present, hanging about her wing tips, and the wand caught it.

Mother Dove felt a quivering beneath her. Oh! Oh, no! No! "Fly away, Terence!"

Terence tried, but the wand made him stick firmly to Mother Dove.

She rose off the nest, praying that the hatching hadn't truly started, that flying the wand away had prevented it. Yet if the hatching wasn't underway, Mother Dove had to return to the egg or it would chill.

But she couldn't return with the wand or the hatching would certainly begin.

The wand tried to force her back, but she had enough magic to resist. She spiraled in the fairy circle, dipping and bucking, trying to throw off Terence.

Minutes passed. The hatching had been arrested, but the egg was cooling.

Terence leaned one way and another, hoping to fall. He braced his feet against Mother Dove's back, pushed off and flapped his wings but didn't rise.

Beck and the animal talents crowded atop the egg, imparting a little warmth, but not enough.

Mother Dove felt a tremor run through Never Land. Its enchantment was fading. The egg was failing.

She flew upside down for a whole minute. The wand kept Terence on her back. She turned right-side up and cawed at it in a language no one had heard before, to no effect. She flew straight at the thick branch of an oak tree.

When she was an inch away she dived.

The branch hit Terence in the chest, knocking him off her back.

He felt a rib crack, but he was glad.

Mother Dove flew to the egg and settled herself, cooing. "Mother is here." The egg was still alive. It would regain its heat. She felt Never Land's magic snap back. "Mother will always be here."

A voice boomed over the fairy circle. "Cute! So many adorable little fairies. Cute! Cute! Cute!"

Dazed, Tink looked around. The voice sounded like Tutupia.

Of course it was the wand, imitating the Great Wandy queen.

Fairies scowled. *Cute, adorable,* and *little* were insults.

Tink flew toward Terence, who was hovering over the fairy circle. He held the wand out to her, but it dragged him away. She flew after him.

"Cute! And so tiny."

The wand made Tink grow.

TWENTY-SIX

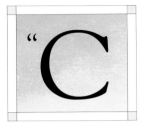"CUTE!" It made all the fairies grow. They grew to six inches tall, eight, a foot. The golden hawk flew from Beck's shoulder to a twig at the top of the hawthorn. He ruffled his feathers, gold side out, to keep the wand from finding him.

The fairies expanded to two feet tall, seven feet, twelve feet, and kept growing. They towered above the hawthorn. Mother Dove became a speck, almost too small to see. The fairies froze, afraid to move and crush her.

Never Land swelled to accommodate the giants. The wand saw the ground move. Hah! It had changed an island.

Rani-bat bleated, Esteemed fairy, please make it stop.

"Cute!"

Terence waved the wand and shouted, his voice booming, "Shrink us back!" As he shouted, his broken rib stabbed at him.

The fairies shrank so fast that for a second their hearts beat high above their heads. Terence felt triumph until he—and everyone—grew again. And shrank again. It hurt in both directions—spread, squeeze, spread, squeeze. Ow! Ow! Ow! Ow!

The wind screamed in Beck's ears as she telescoped up and down. Rani felt like a rubber band. The world rushed by Ree's eyes so fast she had to close them. She swayed and almost toppled. Vidia laughed, trying to grow faster and shrink faster than anyone else. They were all too busy shrinking and expanding to notice how ragged their breathing was, how jagged their heartbeats.

Mother Dove sent her thoughts to the wand. Relax, wand, relax. Why hurry? Be lazy. Relax.

The wand slowed. Fairies paused in their growth and shrinking. Tink was huge at the moment. Terence was small. She took a giant step toward him.

The wand wrenched itself free of Mother Dove's influence and zipped away with him. "Cute fairies!"

Tink shrank again and flew at Terence. The wand forced his arm up. Tink flew higher. Terence's arm grew longer and longer, lengthening faster than Tink could fly. His fingers touched the clouds. She gave up and descended into the hawthorn.

"Cute fairies!" The wand lifted Terence high into an apple tree.

"Vidia!" Tink cried, panting. "I need . . ."

"Yes, darling?"

". . . I need to catch the wand."

"So, sweet?"

"To reverse all the wish—"

"Where is it?"

Tink pointed at Terence in the apple tree.

Vidia flew. It made no difference how big or small she was, she was *fast*. But the wand was faster. The wand zoomed Terence to a pine tree.

Vidia was there, too, but not quick enough to get the wand.

Terence was halfway across the island, at the Wough River. His chest was in agony.

Vidia arrived, too, a beat behind.

Terence, twelve feet tall, was on the pirate ship, but invisible to the pirates. His weight made the ship dip starboard.

Vidia returned to the fairy circle and flew to the nest. "I couldn't help, darling. I'd fly back—" She saw spots before her eyes and fainted.

Prilla saw Vidia fall. Vidia! Stronger than anyone!

Terence was reeling near a dogwood tree. Prilla thought he might faint soon, too.

Rani flew to the dogwood, wanting to do something.

Esteemed fairy, say *please* to the wand. Promise to thank it if it does what you ask.

"Esteemed wand, please let us stop growing and shrinking. I will thank you if you do."

The wand didn't care about politeness.

Furious, Rani spat on it, a torrent of water. The wand was almost washed away, but it stuck to a dry spot on the inside of Terence's pinkie.

Prilla blinked to the mainland and was restored to her normal size. She landed on the desk of a Clumsy girl doing her homework.

"A fairy!"

Prilla pictured Tink at the end of her imaginary tunnel. When she got there, Tink was huge. Prilla threw her arms around Tink's left index finger and blinked.

"Two fairies!"

Tink was her regular size. They both were.

Tink was panting and trembling. "I have to get the wand."

"First catch your breath."

"I'm fine now." But her glow was a mottled green.

"Wait." Prilla wouldn't blink until Tink was tugging her bangs with her usual force. She took Tink's hand and pictured the wand at the end of the tunnel.

Tink and Prilla arrived right at the wand, still held by Terence. Tink's hands joined his on the wand. But before she could begin her repairs, it pulled him away from her.

Prilla blinked Tink back to the mainland.

Tink said, "Get Beck."

Prilla blinked and returned with Beck.

"Three fairies!"

Beck needed a minute to recover.

"I almost had the wand before," Tink said. "If there were two of us, we might hold on to it. Beck?" Her glow flared. "Do you think you have power over the wand?"

"Understanding, not power."

Prilla said, "Understanding is what Mother Dove has."

"Let's blink," Tink said.

This time, when they arrived, they were pressed against the

wand in Terence's hand. The wand pushed the fairies away, but Beck grasped it for a moment and felt its outrage at her touch.

"Terence!" Tink cried, terrified. His face was gray, and he was barely glowing.

He cried out, his voice hoarse, "The leg dust, Tink." He fell out of the air in a faint.

The fairies stopped growing and shrinking. The wand clung to Terence's open hand, but with Terence unconscious it could do nothing more than wriggle.

TWENTY-SEVEN

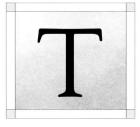INK, BECK, and Prilla reached Terence.
Tink stroked his face. "Wake up! You
can't . . . I don't—"

"The wand!" Prilla yelled. "Take the wand."

Tink and Beck reached for it. Tink grasped it first. Before
Beck could put her hand around it, too, the wand lifted Tink
into the air and pulled her toward Rani. It planned to trick Rani
into taking it, as it had Terence. Rani flew away, fingers splayed,
determined not to grasp it. With one hand, Tink found the leg
dust and sprinkled some on the wand. At the same time, she
thought the command: Slow. Slow.

The wand tried to speed up but slowed down instead.

Rani reached the hawthorn and fainted.

Luckily Tink didn't know. She closed her eyes and focused.
In her mind, she said, This won't hurt, wand. I'm a gentle tinker. We'll do this together. Don't make me grow again.

She flew the wand to the ground, remaining fairy size. Men-
tally she entered the wand.

It was all knotted up inside! There was no serenity,

no smooth flow of impulses, just jumpiness. No wonder the wand was so mischievous. Tink intensified the glow in her hand and used the heat to melt the knots and iron things out.

The wand felt Tink and resisted, clumping itself tighter, pulsing with defiant energy. But Tink knew what she was about. She soothed. She quieted.

Fairies still shrank and grew. Ree scraped herself on a tree trunk and bled heavily. Mother Dove thought Vidia was close to death.

Although she was huge and very dizzy, Beck joined Tink. She put her hand on the wand, too.

Let Beck be her proper size, Tink commanded.

Beck shrank. She closed her eyes and crooned, "Pretty silver wand, funny silver wand . . ."

The wand enjoyed this new fairy's attention, which was merry and sympathetic. The new fairy admired wand mischief, but only mischief that didn't hurt anyone.

The wand didn't care!

Tink delved into the wand's heart. She sprinkled on more leg dust. There. There.

Ah. The wand's heart grew.

And the wand's mind needed sweetening. There. There.

Its spite melted away. Now the wand wanted to please the sympathetic fairy. It felt relaxed and content. It let the fairies stop growing and shrinking.

Prilla turned a double cartwheel. Hooray for Beck and Tink! The nursing-talent fairies went to the injured fairies. The others gathered around the wand. The fairies who had fainted awakened.

Rani sat up.

Are we alive, esteemed fairy?

Terence sat up. "Is Tink safe?"

Beck touched Tink's arm. "Now!"

Tink thought, Wand, good wand, reverse the wishes that fairies and mermaids have made.

Prilla said, "Don't reverse Sara Quirtle!"

But Tink was too absorbed to hear, and she'd forgotten Sara Quirtle. She waved the wand.

It formed obstinate lumps again. Those wishes hadn't been

its fault! Tink smoothed out the new lumps. The wand stopped resisting. It began with the last command it had been given before awakening.

Soop and Pah were at Soop's desk. Pah was telling Soop a mermaid fable. Pah flicked her finger and mouthed the word *the*.

Soop said, "The . . ."

Pah drew two mermaids on Soop's sand slate.

Soop said, "The two friends . . ."

Pah nodded.

Neither of them saw the urn of squid ink vanish from the breakfast tray. They also failed to see the tray itself and everything on it vanish an instant later. Pah wasn't trying to write, so she had no idea that she could again.

Pah pantomimed a breaststroke.

"Swam . . ." Soop said.

". . . away . . ." Pah said, moving her lips carefully.

". . . away . . ." Soop said.

Pah nodded, and then they stared at each other.

"Yooo heard me!"

"I heard you!"

Pah wrote on Soop's slate, "Pah and Soop."

Clink! Ping!

Soop and Pah turned in time to see the glitter vanish from Soop's concealment forest.

"The shells!" Soop cried.

They'd been under the walk-the-plank table, hidden beneath a tablecloth. As they watched, the tablecloth went flat.

Soop shrugged and said, "Oh, well."

Pah frowned. "Yooo were wrong, yooo know, about the song. Its title is 'Squid Swan Song,' not 'Squid Dawn Song.'"

Soop jutted her chin out. "What's a squid swan?"

"Song titles don't have tooo make sense."

"Yes, they dooo! I mean, do!"

The wand was finished with Soop and Pah. The romance dropped out of Tink's feelings for Terence. She didn't notice, since her attention was riveted on the wand. The empty leg-dust pouch fell from her hand.

Vidia's shoulders ached. She flapped her wings and flew a few feet. Nothing had ever hurt so much. Her shoulder blades were exhausted. She hugged the wing polisher next to her. "Darling, I'm so happy."

Terrified, the golden hawk felt himself change. Something was pulling on his wings. His skin felt tight. It was about to burst! His stomach bulged. It was about to explode! Oh, the pressure! The twig beneath him broke.

He flapped his wings. He was big again.

The glory of it!

Ree saw him grow. She should have given the alarm, but she was too pleased to think of it.

He rose above the hawthorn. He could hunt again, for prey large enough to be worthy of him. He could have pounced on a fairy immediately. But since he'd spent so much time with Beck, a fairy meal was unappetizing. He flew away.

Holding his clamshell above the water, Peter sidestroked through the sea toward the pirate ship, carrying out a plan that had been whispered to him by the clamshell.

But . . . but how could a clamshell have planned a pirate raid? Impossible! He must have invented the raid himself. Certainly he had! He let the shell go.

Sara Quirtle was kicking puddle water ahead of her when she became incomplete again. She lowered her foot and stood in the puddle, staring ahead.

TWENTY-EIGHT

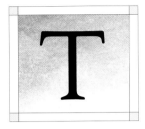

THE WAND paused, aware of Sara Quirtle. A child shouldn't be a stump of wood with stone eyes. A mistake had been made. This wish should stand.

The metal inside the wand formed waves. Tink felt the change but could do nothing. The wand wrenched its power away from her and Beck and restored Sara Quirtle, who kicked the puddle again. She bent over, hands extended, and tried to turn a cartwheel. She fell over with a splash and lay half in the water, laughing.

The wand watched and felt joy for the first time. It jiggled in Tink's and Beck's hands.

After it had completed Sara Quirtle—permanently, so she'd never be incomplete again—it smoothed itself out and went back to reversing wishes.

Rani hovered in the middle of the crowd of fairies surrounding the wand. She should have been on the ground, but she wasn't thinking. Her wings vanished, and she lost her ability to speak and breathe underwater. She fell onto the head of a dairy talent and tumbled to the earth.

Esteemed fairy, where are our wings?

They're gone, esteemed bat. Rani felt almost as sad as she had the first time she'd lost them.

Esteemed fairy, I wouldn't have made the exchange if I had known.

Esteemed bat, I'd fly backward if I could. But we'll be aloft again. There are balloon carriers and there is Brother Dove.

It won't be the same, esteemed fairy.

Esteemed bat, I miss them, too.

I regret your suffering, esteemed fairy.

Rani took this as sympathy. Esteemed bat, something worse is going to happen.

Terrible things have been happening all day, esteemed fairy. What will happen next?

Soop is going to stop liking me, esteemed bat.

That is unimportant, esteemed fairy.

Esteemed bat, it's not!

Soop was alone, lying on her bed, staring up at her coral ceiling. She wished Pah would admit when she was wrong. Once, just once, would be enough. Soop was sure the little fairy wasn't like that. She decided to compose a song for Rani on her next visit.

It should begin, "O, unusual fairy. O, superior fairy. O . . ."

She stopped. She didn't care for fairies. Lesser creatures, every one. She wondered if she might have been mistaken about the name of the squid song, or perhaps the name didn't matter.

Beck whispered, "Tink . . ." She kept in contact with the wand. "It's over."

They felt the wand settle into quiet contentment.

"Mother Dove, it's over," Beck said.

"Prilla . . ." Mother Dove cooed, "blink the wand to the Great Wandies' wand room."

Prilla took the wand. Beck and Tink let go, but stood ready in case new mischief began. The wand only jiggled in Prilla's hands.

Prilla blinked—but not to the Great Wandies.

Sara Quirtle was in her backyard, jumping on a trampoline. She yelled, "My fairy!"

Prilla shouted, "Sara Quirtle!" She flew to the trampoline and started jumping, too.

The wand added to the fun. A kangaroo appeared in the yard and jumped along with them.

Sara Quirtle climbed off the trampoline and ran to the kangaroo, who picked her up and hopped around the yard. Prilla turned cartwheels on the kangaroo's head.

If Tink and Beck had been there, they'd have felt the wand's happy current. They'd have sensed how pleased it was with itself. I'm good! I'm good!

After five minutes of play, when Prilla felt Never Land tugging at her, the kangaroo vanished.

There had always been a Clumsy child or Fairy Haven at the end of Prilla's tunnel, so she wasn't sure she'd be able to blink to the Great Wandies. But she put her trust in Mother Dove, imagined the Great Wandy castle, and blinked.

She was in the castle wand room, flying over the squirming wands. She placed the silver wand atop one of the trays.

Of course it was the finest, biggest-hearted wand the Great Wandies would ever own.

Don't miss the next thrilling adventure!

BY

GAIL CARSON LEVINE

ILLUSTRATED BY

DAVID CHRISTIANA

"GWENDOLYN Jane Mary Darling Carlisle," Grandma whispered, putting down her teacup with trembling fingers, "you are Wendy Darling returned to life."

For her seventh birthday, Gwendolyn had come to breakfast wearing a white dress trimmed with eyelet lace.

"Fetch the scrapbook from my lower bureau drawer, dear," Grandma said. "I want to see."

Gwendolyn returned with a leather scrapbook begun a century before. She set the book on the table and opened it to the middle, where a girl in a lacy white pinafore stared out at them.

Indeed, the two girls looked very alike: heart-shaped faces, level eyebrows, and serious brown eyes that were trained on something beyond, something unseen by anyone else.

In Gwendolyn's case, she was picturing a five-inch fairy flying over the orange-juice pitcher, trailing sparkles of fairy dust. Gwendolyn inhaled the tiger-lily perfume her grandmother always wore. If I go to Never Land, too, she thought, let me meet fairies.

As she blew out her birthday candles, she squeezed her eyes tight and wished, *Peter, come!*

You see, when he remembered, Peter Pan visited the house at Number 14 and brought the latest daughter back to Never Land to do the spring cleaning for him and the Lost Boys. Peter, who was quite behind the times, hadn't yet learned that girls knew boys could clean very well for themselves, at any time of year.

She opened her eyes and saw her father unfastening the silver chain that always hung around her mother's neck.

"The kiss?" Gwendolyn hiccupped, as she often did when she was excited or distressed.

"You're old enough now."

She held her breath as the chain went around her. "I'll take the best care of it."

Of course it wasn't an actual kiss, but an old button made from an acorn. Ignorant Peter had believed it to be a kiss. He'd given it to Wendy soon after they met in the nursery, now Gwendolyn's bedroom. Years later, Wendy's daughter had had the button cast in silver.

Father said, "Every Darling girl has worn the kiss." He blew his nose.

That night, after Gwendolyn's mother read her a fairy tale, Gwendolyn tried to stay awake in case Peter came, but sleep claimed her.

The next night the kiss felt warm through her fairy-print pajama top, even though the evening air was chilly. The yellow curtains stirred in a breeze. The window was never completely shut, even in winter, so Peter might enter.

Gwendolyn closed her eyes and heard the roar of surf, although the harbor was almost half a mile away. Had Peter come?

Her eyes popped open.

No dark silhouette obscured the window. No breath of boy disturbed the air. Only the click of heels against pavement in the street below broke the silence.

She closed her eyes again. . . .

And heard cooing, and saw, on a nest in a hawthorn tree, a dove with glistening white feathers.

Am I dreaming? Gwendolyn wondered.

The dream or vision drew closer. Gwendolyn saw the dove's extraordinary eyes, which were surely filled with feelings and thoughts. Her throat pulsed with the force of her cooing.

"Mother Dove!" someone cried. The voice was breathy, with a ripple of laughter under the words. A glowing figure flew toward the dove, staggering in the air, her arms around a pie almost too big for her to carry.

A fairy?

Excitement brought on Gwendolyn's hiccups. She'd imagined fairies for so long. Stay in sight, she thought, please stay.

The fairy had a tipped-up nose, blue eyes, and red hair tied back in a short braid. She deposited the pie on the nest below Mother Dove's beak. "Dulcie and Tink claim this is the best peach-blueberry pie ever baked."

Tink? Gwendolyn thought. Could she mean Tinker Bell?

Mother Dove pecked the pie. The tip of her beak came up dripping purple juice. "I don't remember when I've tasted such a pie," she cooed. "Beck, tell them how good it is."

Gwendolyn smiled rapturously. This fairy was called Beck. And there was a fairy named Dulcie, who might be friends with Tinker Bell . . . Tink.

Beck dabbed Mother Dove's beak with a tiny napkin. The two continued to discuss the pie and the pie tin, which Tink had repaired. This miraculous pie tin would not permit a crust to be either soggy or burnt, and an unjuicy pie was out of the question.

The kiss cooled. The scene faded. Gwendolyn slid into sleep, but in the morning she remembered everything. At school she reenacted every word and gesture to the delight of her friends Carole and Marcia. Marcia judged Gwendolyn's imitation of a bird to be especially good.

The following night, the kiss remained cool, and Gwendolyn didn't see Never Land. Night after night passed, until she thought the vision had been a one-time occurrence. But two months later, in the morning, when she woke up, the kiss was warm. . . .